FIDDLE
CITY

BY THE SAME AUTHOR

Duffy

FIDDLE CITY

Dan Kavanagh

PANTHEON BOOKS

NEW YORK

Copyright © 1981 by Dan Kavanagh.

All rights reserved under International and Pan-American Copyright Conventions. Published in the United States by Pantheon Books, a division of Random House, Inc., New York. Hardcover edition originally published in Great Britain by Jonathan Cape Ltd., London, in 1981.

Manufactured in the United States of America
First Pantheon Paperback Edition

To Craig and Li

The day they crashed McKay, not much else happened on the M4. At least, not on the stretch between Heathrow and Chiswick; further west, that was somebody else's patch, so who cared? Especially as it was one of those warm, hazy August mornings when the police cars bask like lizards on their special roadside ramps; when those few extra feet above the tarmac permit a careless, unobserved, cap-tilted snooze. And then, perhaps, towards 11.30, the quiet phut and crackle of the FM radio would be eased a bit lower, and finally drowned out by the tiny portable in the blue pocket, tuned to the ball-by-ball.

And the cars weren't giving any trouble either. By ten, the last commuters had vanished east in a swirl of nicotine and bad temper; they wouldn't be back for at least six hours. The commercials, the heavies, the twenty-tonners were un-characteristically well-behaved: something to do with the sun, no doubt. And the civvies: well, on the way to the airport they were too scared of wrecking their holiday to do more than forty; while on the way back, they were so baffled by driving on the left that they often stayed in third gear all the way to the Cromwell Road.

So the blues weren't too pleased when McKay got crashed, when a taxi driver who had seen – well, hadn't really seen anything, just a wreck and a paint smear on the crash barrier – radioed in to his office, who called the local police, who called Heathrow, who transferred it to Uxbridge, who at the third time of asking (England 8 for 1, Boycott bowled Chappell 2: even that bit of the day was going well) managed to raise a drowsily laconic panda crew. Who weren't too pleased with McKay for fucking up their morning. It was almost as if he'd done it deliberately.

7

What was left on the crash barrier might have been paint, but it wasn't. McKay's car had bits of red on it, but not that much. It was a customised Cortina with a tiger motif. At the front, a trompe-l'œil radiator grille whose vertical bars formed the tiger's teeth; along the side, the massed lightning of gold and black jagged stripes; at the back, a tail painted across the bumper, and (McKay's own suggestion, of which he was incontinently proud) a pair of tiger buttocks which met at the point where the special central exhaust protruded. At work, to his face, they called him, as he planned, 'Tiger'; when he wasn't there, they tended to refer to his as The Farting Cat. Sometimes they would watch him drive off, and laugh together at the first gust of blue-grey smoke from between the tiger's buttocks.

McKay left the Western International Cargo Market and headed east towards London. But he didn't drive like a tiger. After a flash bit of foot-down and tyre-squeal as he left work (someone was usually watching, if only a cleaner and his broom), he settled back on the motorway to a steady forty-five. No point burning out the engine before its time. Besides, he liked being in his car – the longer it lasted, the better. Proper little maharajah's palace in here, he used to say. The sound system; the row of miniatures in the 'cocktail cabinet', as he loftily described his glove compartment; the small, padded steering wheel, all black leather and studs; the full Cyril Lord underfoot; sheepskin seats ('The wife makes 'em from the sheep Tiger runs over,' he would explain); even a sheepskin rear-window shelf. On this shelf – another of McKay's favourite touches – lolled a large soft toy. A tiger, of course. McKay was vaguely irritated that its colours didn't match the bodywork, and he'd nearly punched the soft-toy salesman who tried to assure him that the colours were definitely authentic (as if the colours of his Cortina weren't). Still, McKay was able to make a virtue of this whenever anyone mentioned it. 'Tigers come in all colours,' he'd quip, modestly referring to himself as well.

McKay looked up past the too-pale toy and checked the traffic behind him. Just a coach, some twenty yards back. He moved his head a bit and studied his own reflection. The broad, slightly sweaty face, the cupid's-bow mouth, the impassive eyes – they all pleased McKay as much as ever. Vroom, vroom, he thought to himself. Idly, he tugged on the chain around his neck until a thin silver swastika, about two inches square, appeared from beneath his shirt. The leading edges of the emblem had been filed to sharpness: for no particular reason at the time, except that it felt like a good idea. And later, it had proved useful now and then. When he was in the caff, for instance, and that Pakki had started looking at him. Not doing anything, of course – they never dared; they just looked. McKay had dug out a match, reeled in his swastika, and started sharpening the match to a point right in front of the Pakki's face. Then he let the badge dangle and picked slowly at his teeth, all the time staring at this guy. That was one Pakki who didn't bother to finish his sweet.

McKay shifted the swastika in his right hand, selected one of the legs, and began to pick inquisitively at his left nostril with it. That was another reason for keeping to a steady forty-five; though of course, with a racing wheel like this you could drive at seventy with just one little pinkie if you felt like it. As he told people.

He worked methodically at his nostril, occasionally flicking a bogy on to his jeans. A lorry began to overtake him. For a few seconds it was alongside, thumping and shuddering; then it fell back. McKay glanced in the mirror to see where it had gone, but all he saw was the same coach as before; it was a bit closer than last time, maybe ten yards behind.

Typical of fucking lorries, McKay thought. They bang past you going down a hill, swerve in front as soon as they can see six inches of daylight, and then you have to overtake them all over again on the next uphill stretch. Ridiculous; they ought to be made to stay in the slow lane where they belong. Always half-overtaking you and then changing their minds just because there's a one-in-fifty gradient.

9

McKay didn't check on whether it had been a one-in-fifty gradient that had made the lorry fall back. He just assumed it, as anyone else might; and he just happened to assume wrong. Instead, he shifted the swastika in his hand, selected a new leg – he wasn't a dirty bugger, he knew about clean sheets – and began to pick up gently at his right nostril. As he did so, the thump and shudder repeated itself at his shoulder. If McKay hadn't been otherwise occupied, he might have been tempted to have a little game with the lorry, accelerating just enough to keep ahead of it, slowing as the lorry slowed, really getting on its tits. He liked doing that to lorries. But it was a nice morning; McKay was feeling unusually good-humoured; he was on a routine delivery run; and besides, he was picking his nose. So instead, he merely looked ahead (there was a bridge coming up) and then in his mirror – that coach was still there; funny, it was right up his exhaust – and settled back to let the lorry pass.

It was well planned; but then the men hadn't been cheap: they only did one-offs, and they never took rubbish jobs. They were proud of their work; proud, that is, of the way they carried it out. They knew where to steal what they needed; they weren't afraid of wasting a few days on research; and they didn't keep telltale cuttings books on what they did – even though they had, in their own quiet way, made the papers a few times.

The lorry, an articulated eighteen-wheeler, all swaddled in canvas and ropes, drew level with McKay about three hundred yards before the bridge. Gradually it began to inch past, until the back of the trailer was level with the rear offside door of the Cortina; then it seemed just to sit there, straining and burping, unable to get past. Fucking run out of puff again, thought McKay.

The coach, meanwhile, took up even closer order. Anyone following the three vehicles would have concluded that there were only two – a lorry unwisely trying to overtake a coach; the Cortina was completely hidden. And from the front – well, the lorry would hide the car from those directly across from them; and the bridge, they assumed, would take care of the rest. That was what the men had planned; and they were men who weren't cheap.

As the cab of the lorry emerged into the sunlight on the other side of the bridge, the driver twisted the wheel and stamped on the brake at the same time, putting the vehicle into a controlled snake. The back part of the trailer slewed suddenly left and rammed the Cortina in the midriff. 'Just a little boomps-a-daisy,' was how the driver had described it when accepting the first half of the money; but then he was always prone to understatement.

The first effect of just a little boomps-a-daisy was to make the sharpened edge of the swastika rip through the fleshy outside of McKay's right nostril. McKay intended to swear at that point, but events rather got the better of him. Besides, if he had sworn, he might have used up all his best words before something much more unpleasant than a torn nose happened to him; and that would have been a waste.

As the lorry struck the Cortina, the coach pulled out into the middle lane to get clear of whatever might happen. The car was batted diagonally across the hard shoulder. The nearside rear indicator light was the first thing to break against the crash barrier: but then that, compared to the final toll, was about as grave an injury to the Cortina as was McKay's nose to the rest of his body.

Crash barriers work in the way they are intended to, as long as the angle of approach is within a certain range. The Cortina's wasn't. It hit the barrier, stood up on its boot for a second – at which point the doors burst open and McKay was shrugged out – then skipped over the barrier and cartwheeled down an escarpment. McKay himself made a long red trail on the metal barrier in a way that no one could quite understand. It looked, to those who could first be bothered to stop, as if he had been exaggerating terribly: if you were thrown out of your car, why didn't you just land on the barrier and stay there, canted over it like a carpet ready for spring beating? Why did it look as if someone or something had *smeared* the poor fellow all along the barrier? 'Darling, *no* darling . . . *don't* look.' Of course he probably wasn't wearing a seat belt, but even so, it did look a bit much. 'Darling, I *told* you not to look. Darling, are you . . . well, quickly, use that patch of grass over there . . . Oh *Christ*.' Why did one stop for accidents; why didn't one do as all the other fellows did?

No one had seen what had happened. Or rather, no one came forward to say that they had seen what had happened. There was a muted discussion, about an hour later, as an Alitalia DC-8 took off for Palermo, about what exactly had occurred, and those big lorries shouldn't be allowed on the road, I always say, and do you think we should have stopped, and I hope no one took our number, and they couldn't have, they couldn't have known we were watching; but after ten days of a Thomson package, of sun and drink and not too many ruins, the whole incident was more or less forgotten. It was just a bump in the memory, no bigger than the bump in the crash barrier a few yards beyond the bridge.

The police resigned themselves to not getting back to the cricket until it was 63 for 4; it was always 63 for 4 when England batted first against the Australians, so they supposed they could take the rest of the morning as read. The few motorists who had bothered to stop were routinely quizzed, but none of them had seen anything. The drivers of the lorry and the coach turned off at the next junction, and left their vehicles in a lorry park close to the Gunnersbury tube station: they both wanted the District Line, and didn't see why they should have to change, especially after doing a job. They soon forgot the details of their morning's work, and were never required to reflect any further on the crash.

The only people who reflected on it – apart from McKay, of course, as he wheeled himself around in later years – were the two policemen in the panda car and the surgeons at Uxbridge Hospital. As the constables were driving back to their lizard's ramp, one of them switched off the two-way radio and said,

'You know, we could do some business.'

' . . . ?'

'Someone's got to pick up that car, haven't they? I mean, some garage. I mean, it's business, isn't it? It wouldn't be far out of our way to pop round to a garage and tip them off when there's a crash. They'd be bound to be grateful.'

His colleague grunted.

'Been done.'

'Has it? What . . . locally?'

'Not here. Up on the M1, couple of years ago. Big stink. Few early retirements. Didn't work out.'

'Hmm. Well, maybe they were too grabby or something; maybe they got too sure of themselves. I bet we could work it. Just pick the right garage. Not do it too often. Not ask them to be too grateful.'

His colleague merely grunted again, and turned on the two-way radio. It might be worth a think.

Meanwhile, at Uxbridge Hospital, the surgeons were having a more serious think. Should they start on the legs first, or the pelvis? One of the legs looked really messy; it might have to go altogether. On the other hand, with a pelvis you never knew what else you might find until you started digging around. It looked as if there were problems with the back as well. Oh God, that was the trouble with crashes – you never knew where to start. The chief surgeon looked up at McKay's broad, tanned face. Why did they drive so *fast*, for Christ's sake? Oh well, better get on with it. The anaesthetist caught his glance and eased the oxygen mask off McKay's face. The side of the right nostril was slit open to a depth of about half an inch. The bleeding had stopped. Well, at least *that* could wait.

1

Three months earlier Duffy had been sitting over a drink at the bar in the Alligator, trying to decide which of two alarm systems to recommend to a customer: the one which worked better, but on which he got a smaller cut; or the one which worked less well (that electronic eye could be bypassed by a Scotty dog, let alone the fellows with A-levels who were joining the business nowadays), but on which he got a larger cut. Really, he supposed, there was no conflict: he'd disliked the customer so much – the way the fellow had automatically given him a beer while he had sherry (not that Duffy liked sherry), the hoity way he had put Duffy down about the most likely method a burglar would use to break in. Now what he'd do . . .

'Mine's a virgin on the rocks.'

Duffy looked up. A chubby-faced man with pronounced five o'clock shadow was easing himself on to the next stool. He had a pasty complexion and didn't look very fit. Duffy turned back to his whisky. What he'd do was draw up one of his specially complex-looking wiring plans for the old fart's house, recommend the system on which he got a larger cut, shove in a slightly bigger bill than normal, and then hope for the best. It was all luck with burglary, really: if you landed a smart pair of gloved hands in the night, you couldn't stop him; if you landed a trainee, or a shitter, or someone who was only really doing it to get away from the wife, then all you needed was a big white box with a few wires sticking out and they buggered off to the next house.

'I said, mine's a virgin on the rocks, old chum.'

Duffy didn't look back. He wasn't in the mood to be picked up; he certainly wasn't in the mood to spread the drink around. He'd got his bank statement that morning. So he merely raised his glass in the direction of the barman and said, when he came across,

'I think the gentleman on my right wants to buy himself a drink.'

He heard a chuckle, then:

'Virgin on the rocks, same again for my friend here, whatever it is he's got his fist wrapped around, the name's Leonardo.'

Duffy continued to gaze into his whisky. If chubby-chops wanted to buy him a drink, that was up to chubby-chops. He turned, and caught a look of scurrying anticipation from the next stool.

'Leonardo . . . virgin . . . oh, forget it. Barman, put a vodka in that, will you. Large one.' Then he turned back to Duffy. 'Pity, that would have been an easy round for you. I'm not a cheap date after the first.'

'You're not a date,' said Duffy.

'Eric Leonard,' said the newcomer.

'Duffy,' said Duffy.

'Anything else? *Sir* Duffy.'

'There's a Nick.'

'There usually is. My dear Nick,' Leonard repeated the name needlessly, in a mildly ingratiating way. Duffy almost didn't recognise himself. At work he was Duffy; to his close friends he was Duffy; the only people who called him Nick were acquaintances who didn't know – or weren't allowed – better. So that was all right for the moment.

'And you shall call me Eric.'

'I'll think it over.' Duffy was always suspicious of people without proper surnames. Two Christian names: it wasn't right; it wasn't . . . neat.

Duffy wondered what Leonard wanted. Apart from going to bed with him of course. Which was a long way from being a certainty. Mostly you went down to the Alligator so as not to go home alone – that stood to reason; but sometimes you just went for the atmosphere, a bit of drinking company, and then, with a 'some other time, perhaps', you were on your way. That was one of the things Duffy liked about the Alligator. It wasn't a hard raunch club; it wasn't a place where people came Concording out of the closet in a splatter of supersonic bangs; it wasn't a place for clones – the lumberjack shirt, the little tache, the logger's jeans; it wasn't a place for leather and chains and 'Hang on, I'll just go to the toilet and grease my fist'. It was a quiet, neat place for quiet, neat people like Duffy. It was even, he supposed, a bit middle-class.

Which was why Eric struck Duffy as a slice of rough. The pushy manner, the double entendres – that was so out of date, all that stuff; as out of date as bottom-pinching. You may be gay, Duffy thought to himself, but that's where you start from, not where you end up. Duffy wasn't a prude, but he might have been a bit of a puritan. He wondered what sort of job Eric did; but he didn't wonder hard enough to ask.

Eric, for his part, had put Duffy in the same category. He hadn't been to the Alligator before, and found it depressingly conventional. You might as well be in a singles bar in midtown Manhattan, he thought. All those blue blazers, and striped shirts, and *ties* for God's sake. And in the middle of them, this shortish fellow in a blouson with a big plastic zip up the front, and a polo-neck sweater and a longish brushcut. As he slid on to the barstool, Eric had noted the broad, strong face with a slightly small, tight mouth; the hands too were strong, with stubby, square-ended fingers. The first time Duffy turned towards him, Eric noted the gold stud in the left ear lobe. You'll do me, he thought, you'll do me, my nice little slice of rough.

Except that he didn't. When Eric finished what had turned into a bloody Mary he leaned across and said,

'Well, Sir Duffy, shall we mount up?' the fellow had simply put down his glass, shaken his head and replied, 'No.'

And Duffy had wandered home, depressed by the thought of his bank statement, and depressed by the way he'd very nearly not said No.

Eric, meanwhile, was regretting the drink he'd had to pay for. He had a rule about drinks: Leonard's Law, he called it to himself. Always buy more drinks than are your due for those richer than yourself; but sponge off those poorer than you. That way, both lots respected you.

The funny thing was, it hadn't worked with this Duffy fellow. He hadn't seemed to need to be sponged off. Some psychological hangup, no doubt. Maybe, Eric thought, he ought to have asked the fellow more questions about himself. They always liked that.

A fortnight later, Leonard called in at the Alligator again. This time, when he spotted Duffy, he altered his act a bit, played it more ordinary, even went so far as to ask him what he did.

'I run a firm.'

'Ah, what line of business?'

'Security.'

'Would I have heard of the firm?'

'You heard of Duffy Security?'

'No.'

'Then you wouldn't have heard of it.'

Eric was suddenly a bit keener than before to get off with Duffy. He'd fucked a policeman once, but never anyone in the security business. He had a vague, half-formed ambition to sleep with someone from every trade and profession (there were exceptions, of course, like bankers and stockbrokers and barristers; but then you weren't a left-wing journalist for nothing: sometimes you simply couldn't help running up against your principles). Fucking a security man; that was something new. Though of course he didn't tell Duffy.

And in reply, Duffy didn't let on that he was only a one-man firm; that his office was an answerphone; that his van was 'F' registration; that he didn't even have a dog. Not that he ever needed a dog; it was just that some people thought they gave status. But Eric didn't cross-question him on the details; his curiosity was more or less exhausted by now. Instead he asked:

'Can you give me a lift home?'

And Duffy replied,

'All right.'

In the event, they went to Duffy's flat, the bottom half of a semi in Goldsmith Avenue, Acton. At first the flat struck Eric as very neat; then he realised that it was less neat than empty. What there was by way of furniture and decoration was tidily enough arranged; but the effect bordered on the monkish.

'You been burgled or something?' he asked, thinking that this was the sort of remark a security man might be amused by. But Duffy didn't reply. Instead he pointed at the bathroom and said,

'Watch in there.'

'I beg your pardon?' What was he meant to watch?

'*Put* your watch in there.'

Ah. Well, if that was how he ran things. Eric wandered into the bathroom and saw a square Tupperware box with a label on it. The label said 'Watches'. He unpeeled his strap and dropped the watch in; then, puzzled but feeling distantly indulgent, he unsnapped his silver name-bracelet with the 'EL' almost camouflaged by engraved curlicues, and he dropped that in afterwards. Maybe it was like giving up your valuables to the groundsman. He'd have to ask Duffy about that.

If he had, Duffy might have told him about his ticking phobia. But Eric didn't ask. When he got to the bedroom his host was already between the sheets. Eric vaguely looked around to see where to put his clothes. Duffy's own were nowhere to be seen. Tidy again. Oh well, he thought, it was all part of meeting the people.

The next morning Eric left in a normally ambiguous frame

of mind. He'd added a security man to his list, that was something. On the other hand, fucking Duffy was much like fucking someone who wasn't a security man: if you closed your eyes, you wouldn't find yourself thinking, I am clearly in the hands of a man skilled in cash transfers, alarm systems and personnel screening. You wouldn't think that. So, while in one way it made every difference to Eric that Duffy was a security man, it also made none at all. Well, that bit of wrong-footing was nothing new about sex, he thought.

He'd sort of quite liked Duffy – as far as one did on such occasions (and liking was often alloyed with relief that it had all passed off O.K. and hope that there wouldn't be any bacterial after-effects). He'd even gone so far, on leaving, as to say,

'See you around.'

'No,' Duffy had replied politely, and Eric found himself thinking, I didn't know I was *that* bad. But Duffy's negative had no connection with the night before; it only had connection with Carol, and events of four years ago, and a lot of past history that he certainly wasn't going to spill to one-nighters.

And there were only one-nighters in Duffy's life at the moment. One-nighters of both sexes, as it happened; but however erotically competent they were, or clean, or interesting, or even good old-fashioned nice, they only got to drop their watches into his box once. Carol, ex-colleague from West Central police station, ex-girlfriend (no, still girlfriend, sort of), and also ex-fiancée (no, not quite: she'd asked him, and he'd said No) – she was the only exception; and a bitter, wry exception at that. The one person Duffy wanted to succeed with in bed; the one person with whom he automatically failed – had failed so often now that he no longer tried. Potency with Carol, Duffy had long decided, was an idiot's mirage. You might as well believe in Heaven.

'Mine's still a virgin on the rocks,' a familiar voice whispered in his ear at the Alligator three months later. 'Where've you been, Sir Duffy?'

Duffy signed at the waiter, and interpreted.

'Tomato juice, lots of ice.'

'Oh well, old thing, if you're buying . . .' Eric retained the waiter with a flick of the eyebrow. 'Dunk a couple of vodkas in it while you're about it.'

'No, you're paying,' said Duffy, stubborn about being taken in by that sort of trick.

'God, you don't guard cash transfers for nothing, do you?' Eric gave a theatrical groan. 'Anyway, I'll come straight to the point.'

'No,' said Duffy. 'I said not again, didn't I?' Why did people always think No meant Yes, soon?

'Wait. Waity-wait. Job. Want a job?'

'Maybe.'

'That's why I've been looking for you.'

'I'm in the book.'

'Yes, but it's much more fun sitting here being bought a drink than talking to your secretary down the phone, isn't it?'

Duffy let one of the two remarks pass, but picked up on the other.

'You're still buying.'

'A friend of a friend . . . is having a little trouble.'

'That doesn't surprise me.' There was something about the pallid face and the buoyant manner which irritated Duffy. Be one or the other, he thought.

'Always a little tart, eh?' (Duffy let that one pass too.) 'A little thieving seems to be going on at his establishment.'

'There's this quite useful branch of the civil service they've set up, you know. It's called the police.'

'Well, obviously he has his reasons.'

'What are they?'

'It's a small establishment – half a dozen or so employees. Good relationship all round, just happens to be one rotten apple. Now if he went to the police they'd come clumping in with their great boots, stir everything up, put everyone under suspicion, wouldn't they?'

'They might stop the stealing.'

'So he thought, get someone private in, let him sniff around. Can't do any harm, can it?'

'No. It can only cost money. Why did you suggest me?'

'Well, you run a security firm, don't you?'

'That's not how you know me.'

'No, but we must stick together, mustn't we?'

Ah, thought Duffy: gays as the new masons – is that what's happening? Would he have to learn a new handshake soon? He was irritated. Once you didn't need solidarity, you resented its offer.

'Tell me more.'

'His name's Hendrick. He runs a transport and storage business out of Heathrow. He's been losing rather more stuff than he cares for lately.'

'How would he explain me? I'm not much good leaning on a mop.'

'One of his men just had a car crash. He'll be off for some time.'

'Convenient. What do I do?'

'He'll tell you.'

'I charge . . .'

'Duffy,' Eric cut in, 'I'm not a fucking broker. You fix that up with him. I don't care what you earn. You want the job, go and see him.' Eric was annoyed. First Duffy acted as if he expected to be raped; then he got all uppity. Eric scribbled on the top of a newspaper. 'This is his London office. Ring up, say you've called about the papaws.'

'The what?'

'The papaws. As in fruit. Tropical. It's a code, Duffy. It's not a good idea, we thought, for you to ring up and say you're calling about sorting out the thefts.'

'I get.'

'I hope so.' Eric began to slide off his barstool. He felt he'd been misjudged. He certainly hadn't taken Duffy's No to mean Yes, soon. He'd only taken it to mean Perhaps, in a bit.

'Oh, two things.'

'Yes?'

'Who's your friend?'

'. . .?'

'The friend who's the friend in "a friend of a friend".'

'Oh, it's not relevant.'

'How do you know?'

'Because *he* hasn't been stealing from his friend's firm, that's why. And what's the second thing?'

'Oh – don't go without paying for the drinks.'

Duffy sat opposite Roy Hendrick in an office the size of a bus shelter just off the Euston Road. His secretary had a room the size of a large refrigerator. Hendrick didn't seem very comfortable. Perhaps he wasn't that familiar with his office – perhaps it was only here for tax reasons, or to impress customers by appearing to show a London end to the business. Or perhaps Hendrick was uncomfortable for some other reason; maybe he was lying to Duffy. Clients often did.

Hendrick, a fleshy, saturnine man with dirty blond hair and a flapping suit which might just have been handed on from someone else, explained the problem.

'I'm not an angel, Mr Duffy, and I don't expect other people to behave like angels. It's just that there are limits.'

'Uh-huh.'

'If you get the removers in, when you shift house, you expect to lose a bit, don't you? I mean, if you're sensible, you pack up the stuff you really care for and take it yourself, and then don't get too surprised if you suffer a small attack of removers' perks in the course of the job. That's the way it is, isn't it?'

'If you say so.' The only removers Duffy had ever come across had been burglars. At his last flat he'd been burgled twice: the second time, they'd taken everything, his pile of sixpences and his electric kettle included; they'd even taken his pot plant. He'd been left with a few ashtrays, a bed and a carpet. That scarcely warranted hiring a pantechnicon when he moved flats.

'Well, the freight business is rather the same. You expect to lose a bit if you ship by air. It goes through so many hands, has to be opened by customs – well, there are more temptations than Adam ever had, if you follow the expression.' (Duffy didn't look a bookish fellow to Hendrick.) 'And you know what they say about Heathrow?' Hendrick paused. It was clear from Duffy's expression that he didn't know what they said about Heathrow. 'No one who works there ever needs to buy fresh fruit and veg. They tell me there's scarcely a greengrocer within miles. Anyone around there who catches his wife trying to *buy* a pound of apples or whatever practically has her committed on the spot.'

Hendrick stared at Duffy, inviting vague complicity towards the opposite sex. Duffy looked blank. Hendrick stared briefly at the gold stud in Duffy's left ear. He felt like giving it a tweak, if only to make the man say something. Eventually Duffy did speak, if reticently.

'Uh-huh.'

'What do you mean by *uh-huh*?'

'You've been losing apples, is that what you're saying?'

'No. Well, yes, sort of, but that's beside the point. I've been running the business for five years. Always accepted a certain percentage of pilfering. There's almost an unspoken agreement at times: it helps them bump up their wages, I charge it to the insurance and turn a blind eye. Not worth going into.'

'But recently . . .'

'But recently, about once a month or so, it's got out of hand: a really big dip. Something I can't go along with.'

'Like?'

'Caseload of calculators. Half a dozen furs. Two crates of smoked salmon.'

'You carry only luxuries?'

'Not really. We freight a pretty mixed bag; bit of everything. But you don't shift stuff by air unless it's valuable, or perishable, or has to be shipped quickly because of the state of the market. We don't get many crates of garden furniture or dried pigfeed, if that's what you're asking, no.'

'So how do you get me in?'

'You can take McKay's place. Poor old McKay,' Hendrick added, as if confirming compassion; but the repetition made it seem artificial (and perhaps it had never been very sincere in the first place). 'Nearly wrote himself off. Did write his car off. Very nice car.' In the last comment at least Hendrick was indubitably sincere.

'What do I do?'

'Bit of everything: we're a small firm. Everyone mucks in. Bit of driving, bit of humping things about, bit of helping Mrs Boseley.'

'. . .?'

'Oh, she runs the shed for me. First-class woman, keep you on your toes.'

'Wears furs a lot, does she?'

Hendrick looked up, the saturnine face pulling itself lethargically into an expression of shock. Before it got there, Duffy flashed an uncommon smile. 'Just a little joke, Mr Hendrick. Have to ask, don't we?'

'You report to her as soon as you can start. Tomorrow?'

'The day after. I charge twenty-five a day.'

'Yes, well that's about what McKay was getting, so that'll be all right.'

'No, that's on top of McKay's salary. If I'm doing two jobs I want two paypackets.'

They haggled. As usual, Duffy opened firmly, then lost a bit of interest and ended up conceding enough to make him feel cross with himself afterwards. Still, he was getting one and a half times his going rate, and he wouldn't mind shifting a few sacks now and then. Especially if that included not going to the greengrocer's for a few weeks.

2

'Up the bum?' repeated Duffy incredulously.

'Up the bum.'

Duffy's sphincter tightened involuntarily. Willett kept his smile within himself; funny how that always got to them. He went on,

'Four up the back, three up the front. Or it may have been the other way round. Not that it makes much difference. Nice girl, too. Well, niceish – you know, posh as usual. Time was, of course, when any bit of posh would go straight through, or give you the sharp edge if you dared to ask her if you could possibly examine that tiny *valise*' (he pronounced it in a mimsy, fake-upper-class way) 'which just happened to have fifteen furs poking out of the side. Nowadays, a bit of posh, travelling alone, bit unsteady on her feet, and we know the full story before she's even started telling us. These girls, think they're so grown-up, go off round the world, meet this *ebse-lutely sweeeet* Persian, or Arab, or something, fall for him – sometimes he's fed her a bit of coke, but often not, they do it for love nearly all the time – and before they know where they are they're teetering off the plane with half a dozen condoms of heroin up them. Well if you've had *that* up you for, what, say, twelve hours, you know about it, don't you? And some of these poor girls – these foreign gents they fall for aren't stupid, I mean they know we watch planes from the obvious places, so they make them do great detours round the world before fetching up here – some of these girls have had half a dozen up them for thirty-six hours. I mean, they look as if they've just got off a horse. Silly stuffers.'

'That what they're called?'

'Stuffers – yes. Silly girls. Lots of them are quite sweet. "What will *Memmy* say . . . And Abdul – I did *so* adore him." Silly stuffers. And of course we never do get the Abduls. Sometimes they send someone to ride shotgun with the girls – make sure they don't have a bright idea and dump it all down the toilets on the plane.'

'So who gets it out?'

'Eh?'

'Who searches them – the stuffers?'

'Up there? No, it's not on. You have to wait for it to come out. I mean – it's an assault against the person or whatever. We can strip-search them, but we can't probe. Thou shalt not probe.' Willett let his smile come out this time.

'So what do you do?'

'Whip them down the special stuffers' toilet.'

'. . . ?'

'It's a room we put them in when we think they're stuffing. Bed, couple of chairs, and at one end this toilet on a sort of throne. Raised up, looks quite posh. The bowl has a plastic lining, like what the wife puts in the pedal bin. I mean, it's obvious what we're there for: the toilet's the sort of central feature of the room, and anyway we usually tell them what we suspect. And then one of us just sits there and waits for them to get on with it. After all, if they want to prove they're *not* stuffers, there's an easy way, isn't there? Bit smelly, but easy.'

'How long do you have to wait?'

'Oh, days, sometimes. The trouble is, you can't take your eyes off them either. If you nod off you know what they'll do.' Duffy didn't. 'They shit it out and then swallow it again.'

Duffy gulped, and gazed queasily at his chocolate éclair.

'They do *that*?'

'If it's that or seven years, I reckon you might bite the bullet.'

Duffy reckoned so too, though he didn't care to give the choice very much thought.

'It must be boring, all that waiting.'

'Well, it is. If we were in Hong Kong or somewhere like that, we could give them Ex-Lax in their coffee and then Bob's yer uncle. But not here – that'd be another assault, giving them the Ex-Lax. So we just have to wait, and we hold them as long as it takes. And then when they finally see they can't leave without first being excused, it's on with the rubber gloves, clothes-peg on the nose, and think of England.'

'You sure there's nothing in this coffee?'

'Just a little persuader or two. You see, I want you to take these packages of fruit-gums out to Baghdad.' Willett grinned. He rather fancied finishing off Duffy's éclair for him. 'Oh, and in case you're wondering, the record for a stuffer is fifty-five. Includes back and front, of course. And the record for a swallower is 150. That's one thing you won't find in the *Guinness Book*.'

Duffy grinned back at him. Willett was a nice old boy; well, not that old – fiftyish. His hair was thinner now than when they had first met, but he was still the same stocky, crease-faced, garrulous old bugger Duffy remembered. He had the face of your best friend's favourite uncle – which was perhaps why he was such a good customs officer. You couldn't lie to your friend's favourite uncle: or if you did, you felt so guilty that it showed. Willett had been a senior officer since Duffy had first come across him in the line of business; and he'd been in the service long enough to still think of himself by the abandoned but cherished title of Waterguard.

They were sitting over coffee in Terminal One's Apple Tree Buffet. Behind Duffy's back was the excuse for the name: a dead tree, fifteen feet high, decorated all over with red and green fairy balls. Above his head the main departure board occasionally rattled out the summonses of the afternoon; the same information was repeated here and there on pairs of television screens. Every thirty seconds or so an instruction boomed calmly over the public address, and teas were abandoned half-drunk. 'Final call' was a popular phrase in these parts: it rang in Duffy's ears like a *memento mori*. He bet there were retired pilots who named their sunset bungalows 'Final Call'.

Only Willett's presence prevented Duffy giving way to medium-grade paranoia. He hated airports. He hated planes too. Both, doubtless, because he hated Abroad. He didn't hate foreigners – at least, not more than most people – but he did hate where they came from. Duffy had never been abroad, of course, but he knew without going that some form of craziness would be bound to strike over there. And so he hated everything that reminded him of the ease with which this dreadful fantasy could be made real. The sight of planes in the sky made him duck; a British Airways bus cruising harmlessly along the Cromwell Road filled him with anxiety. He didn't even like meeting stewardesses – he felt in some obscure way that they might kidnap him, and he'd wake up gagged and bound in the cargo hold of a nose-diving DC-10. And that was another thing about planes: they crashed; they killed you. If Duffy were king, all aircraft would have painted along the side of the fuselage: 'THIS PLANE CARRIES A GOVERNMENT HEALTH WARNING'.

There was another thing about this place, this Heathrow. It was like being in a foreign city. People stopped being English here – even if they were English. They banged into you with cases and didn't apologise. They pushed in front of you in queues. They shouted. They unashamedly expressed emotion at the departure gate. They were already competing with foreigners at being foreign. And all around there were these tiny Asian women in brown smocks: carrying trays, pushing mops, clearing ashtrays, walking gracefully in and out of the toilets. Most of them were so small they made Duffy feel full-sized; many of them struck him as quite old; they never spoke, except to each other, and then in a tongue from Abroad. The only thing that made you think it wasn't Abroad were the signs everywhere and the unnervingly calm-voiced announcements on the public address. But even that didn't mean you had to be in England. As a tiny Asian woman removed Duffy's tray he realised what the place felt like: a thriving outpost of Empire, with an efficient local slave population.

'What's it about, Duffy?' Willett was doing his avuncular look. That was O.K. by Duffy. He liked Willett. And in any case, customs officers didn't count the same as stewardesses: after all, they were there – or so it felt to Duffy – to discourage people from going abroad, to make things nasty for them, vaguely to represent the disapproval of authority. Not at all like stewardesses.

'I don't know yet. I'm just sort of on the scout. I've got a job starting tomorrow in the cargo market. Bit of thieving. Don't really know any more. Just thought I'd remind myself a bit of the place – and keep up with you, of course. I don't have much call to come here normally.'

Willett creased his face again; he knew about Duffy's phobias.

'Thieving's not much of a surprise. After all, this is Fiddle City, Duffy.'

'Uh-huh.'

'I mean, the papers, and the judges, they call it Thiefrow, don't they? But the thieving – that's only a small part of it. It's Fiddle City, Duffy, this place – Fiddle City.'

'Uh-huh.'

'It's true. What does Joe Public think? Joe Public thinks it's all about smuggling, doesn't he? He thinks this place is all about sneaking the extra bottle of duty free, or asking to see the receipt for your camera; and then occasionally there's this great boogie comes hoofing it through the door, and there's something about him that makes us think, bingo, he's the one, and he has this big leather cap on his head, and we take it apart, and in the little button on the top we find a diamond, or a tab of L.S.D., or a microdot with the secrets of the atom bomb. That's what Joe Public thinks, isn't it? Joe Public's a bloody muggins.'

'Uh-huh.'

'It's a city, Duffy, it's a city.' Willett was settling back and getting launched. 'It's as big as Newcastle, and the population changes every day. Think of it like that. So of course you get your smuggling, but that's only the speciality of the place. You get all your other city crimes as well, and you get your sharper operators because they're smart enough to see why it's different from a normal city. It's different because it's very rich, because it's open twenty-four hours of the day, and because lots of the people who are here are only thinking of getting home, and as long as they get home without losing *too* much, then that's O.K.

'There's the smuggling, sure. Then there's the thieving. Then there's the armed robbery. Then there's the pickpockets, and the forgers, and the pushers, and most of all the fiddlers. There's so many fiddles, Duffy, you wouldn't believe. You know what they say . . . '

'About the fresh fruit and veg? I heard it.'

'Well, that's one you've heard. You've probably heard about the cowboys at the cab rank too – three hundred quid to Birmingham and then drop you at the first motorway sign to Brum and let you walk.'

'Uh-huh.'

'Do you know the car park one?' Willett felt competitive, needing to impress Duffy with a really good fiddle.

'No.'

'Ah. Car park.' Willett waved a vague hand in the right direction. 'Short-stay car parks, long-stay car parks. O.K.?'

'O.K.'

'Long-stay park much cheaper, but it's a bit further away. You have to take the bus to the terminal. Dump your car, leave the keys, fill in a form saying when you'll be back to collect it, fly off to the sunshine and the señoritas. What happens? Little car-hire firm springs up. No questions asked, and a lot cheaper than your Hertz or your Avis. Who's going to remember the mileage on his car all the way through a lovely holiday? And if

31

they do, well, you can always turn the clock back, can't you?'

'Sounds foolproof. Is it still working?'

'No, silly cowboys had too many crashes. Got themselves closed down. As far as anyone can tell, of course.'

'It's a good fiddle,' Duffy said admiringly.

'First-class while it lasted. Pity they made a Horlicks of it.'

Duffy nodded. He knew the feeling; it was common to all branches of law enforcement. After an initial period when you wanted to arrest everyone for everything – when every Troops-Out badge or half-flicked V-sign appeared to be Conduct Liable to Cause a Breach of the Peace – you settled into a realisation that you'd never catch everyone, you'd never clear up everything. You caught quite a lot of people because they were stupid, and you came to despise them for taking up a trade they were so ill-equipped for; you caught quite a lot of people because you were lucky; and you caught quite a lot of people because you worked very hard and wanted very much to catch them. Murderers, child molesters, that sort of thing – you hated them. But there were some crimes and some criminals you couldn't help admiring, even liking. Crimes which had a lot of thought put into them, which were very well executed, and which hurt nobody – or virtually hurt nobody. You almost didn't want to catch whoever was doing it because it gave you something close to pleasure: and if they then went and made a Horlicks of it, you felt irritated with them; as if, by letting you catch them, they'd somehow let you down.

'How do you know who to search?' It was a question everyone asked Willett sooner or later.

'Trade secret. No, I'll tell you. Mixture of science and nose, that's what it is. And I mean literally nose sometimes. We've got one officer here, got a better nose than his dog. True, I swear it. We'll be going over a cargo with a dog – the dog's meant to sniff the cannabis, but this mate of mine often gets there first. Tells the dog where to sniff. Dog jumps up and down, wags his tail and gets another steak dinner. Amazing nose.'

'But would you search me, for instance?'

'Depends. Sometimes we get tip-offs, of course. Sometimes we take a little peek at the suitcases before they come up on the carousel – that helps us a bit. And we'll watch you, often from the moment you get off the plane. Not *you*, necessarily, but some people. And don't trust any mirror, by the way, don't trust any mirror.'

'Doesn't sound as if you'd stop me.'

'No, maybe we wouldn't. But then every officer's different. If you don't have any information, then you're down to your nose. There are two sorts of nose – what I call scientific nose, and what I call random nose. Scientific nose is when you look for guys who are nervous, or haven't got what feels the right amount of luggage. Sometimes their case might come up first on the carousel – we can arrange these things – but they pretend not to notice it, and then only grab it when about half the other passengers have already taken theirs. Well, you'd turn *him* over. That's what I call scientific nose.

'Now random nose is different for everyone. For instance, I stop everyone with a raincoat slung over their left shoulder. Sounds silly, doesn't it? But you need some sort of random factor to operate on, if only to keep you on your toes yourself. I know officers who stop people wearing white suits; if you ask them to explain, they say it's for really deep psychological reasons – they reckon the guy puts on the white suit to make other people think he's pure and innocent and not trying to get away with something. Of course, often the guy's got his white suit on because he doesn't want to get it creased in his suitcase, or thinks it might get nicked, or wants to try and pick up a stewardess. But the officer thinks there's more to it, or persuades himself that way, when really he's just using random nose. It varies: some officers stop people who aren't smiling, or who are smiling, or blond men, or bald men, or men who are with girls the officers fancy. That's often just to get a longer look at the girl, or it may be jealousy after a hard night on the feet and getting the pip at seeing these swankies jetting in from L.A. I can't say I blame them.'

'Do you search the crews?'

'Of course. That's rummage – that's what we call it. I was on rummage last week. We turned them upside down as usual. Didn't find much – though it's done to deter as much as to find stuff.'

'Anyone you can't search?'

'Diplomatic bag. Though there are always ways.'

'Such as?'

Willett smiled.

'Send in a ferret, of course.' Duffy should have known better than to expect a straight answer. 'No, but the short one is, Duffy, like I said before, this is Fiddle City. No one's above the law, and a hell of a lot of people are below it.'

Duffy didn't like to speak his next thought, so instead he merely cocked an eyebrow towards his friend.

'Cheeky sod.'

Duffy recocked his eye.

'Well since you ask, no, not in my experience. Not here. There was a bit of a rumble down at Gatwick a few years ago – the odd backhander was finding its way through from pilots of an airline we won't mention. But here? Half of them are Scottish, which is a good start, and I say that as an Arsenal supporter. No. It's much more than their job's worth, you'd get a hell of a sentence, and it'd be very hard to pull off. Though sometimes I can see it happening: the haul of a lifetime – you might just be tempted. And if anyone was tempted, I'd blame Mrs Thatcher. No, really, I would.'

'I always thought you were a Tory.'

'Am. Voted for the lady. Don't tell the wife,' Willett looked conspiratorial, 'but I fancy her a bit. All those nicely tailored suits. I'd let her through any day: she could come up my green channel and no questions asked. *But* – the lady did a terrible thing: she stopped the reward system. I'm sure it wasn't Mrs T.

herself, *personally*; but the next time the little civil servant who thought it was a good idea comes through here, he's going to get the linings taken out of his suits and no mistake.'

'You voting Tory again next time?'

'Take more than that, Duffy. But you know, they talk about incentives – what incentive have we got now? Why do they stop anything that works, Duffy?'

'That's not my sort of question.' They stood up together, and Duffy shook Willett's hand. 'I'll maybe come and see you again in a week or two.'

'Any time. Who knows, I may be round your shed for a rummage before you can say Jack Robinson.'

'Well, you don't know me if you do.'

'Sure. Watch out for illegal golf clubs, Duffy. They're sort of long and thin and made of metal and come in bags.'

'I'll keep my eyes skinned.'

'Keep them skinned for the cowboys as well. I mean that. The cowboys round here aren't any nicer than the cowboys anywhere else. Very short on morals, some of them.'

'Got you.'

And Duffy headed off through the raucous bazaar of this strange imperial city.

Next day, before leaving for work, he rang Carol and asked her round that evening. She said she couldn't make it; as always, the news gave him a stab. He didn't ask; she didn't explain; that was the deal. At one time she used to tell him when she was going to do things she knew he wouldn't mind about – go to the pictures with a fellow-W.P.C.; or visit her aunt – but this only made him think that when she didn't explain she must be going to the Ritz with Paul Newman, or making half a dozen pornographic films that evening. So they went back to the original system of her not saying, and his not asking. She'd come the following night instead.

He guessed his clothes for Hendrick Freight: a denim jacket

which looked as if it were made from separate patches but wasn't (Duffy felt cheated when Carol had pointed out that it was done with false seaming); his oldest jeans, with authentic patches on the knees; desert boots. That should do it.

As he climbed into his van he reflected yet again how smart he'd been not to have it plastered with business slogans saying DUFFY SECURITY and pictures of red skulls and crossbones or whatever. Some firms worked like that: high visibility, they called it. He did, actually, have a board with DUFFY SECURITY painted on it: there were rubber suckers on the back and it could be stuck to the side of the van if he was going anywhere on official business. He'd originally had two such signs, one for each side of the van, but he lost one on a trip to Barking. He must have been producing a poor quality of spit that day.

So: his clothes were O.K., the van was O.K. (that's to say, it had started), the interview was rigged and so presumably would be O.K. (Hendrick had said the best story for Mrs Boseley would be that Duffy had done a lot of odd jobs around his house for him and was now looking for something permanent). He was driving along the M4 in the opposite direction to most of the commuter traffic, so *that* was O.K. The only thing which wasn't O.K. was that he was going to have to keep tracking back to Heathrow every day and listen to the aircraft whining in pain, and watch them taking off at a ludicrously untenable angle, and it would be just his luck if one of them decided to stall into the freight area during the next few days.

His was a rational unease. If you worked around airports and *didn't* fret, you were the odd one, Duffy had long ago decided. Across to his left, a long slow morning line of jumbos was queuing up to land, sticking parallel to the M4. (It was obviously the only way they knew how to navigate. 'Well, personally, I take the A205 through Mortlake . . . ' 'Oh, I'm much more of a North Circular man myself . . . ' That was all the pilots ever talked about.) The planes kept a mile astern of one another, which was a criminally inadequate distance, as even Duffy could see. And they were flying so slowly – barely overtaking him. It was probably some competition to see who could go the slowest without stalling.

Look at it this way, Duffy told himself. The sooner you find out who's nicking Hendrick's stuff, the sooner you can stop worrying about a DC-10 turning into a Stuka, or about a cubic yard of frozen pee landing on your head from 20,000 feet. Fair enough. He turned off the M4 at Junction Three, ducked his head automatically as he cut across the flight path of the jumbos, and skirted the perimeter of the airport.

Freight was handled on the south side of Heathrow. Inside the fence was the bonded area: there, the sheds belonged to individual airlines, who were responsible for cargo until it had cleared customs. Then they handed it either direct to the importer, or to one of the gaggle of freight agents just outside the fence.

Hendrick Freight stood in one of the less fashionable areas of this subsidiary cargo market. Smarter forwarding agents were clustered under one roof in a modern shed close to the road. The security man on the gate let Duffy through after a brief phone call, and directed him to Hendrick Freight. It was a high, airy shed – Duffy hoped the job didn't drag on until the winter – with side walls of yellow-painted breeze-block and an arching, corrugated tin roof. Bundles of goods lay on rust-coloured, triple-tiered racks. Large red numbers hung above each storage bay.

As he stood there a yellow fork-lift truck suddenly whined past and nearly ankle-tapped him with one of its two flat metal prongs. Better watch out, thought Duffy. Collect one of those in the leg and you'll be catching up on a lot of reading before you know where you are. He began to walk slowly up the length of the shed. Neolithic strip lighting lurked in the roof, and had to be helped out by the occasional bare, hanging bulb. Weighing machines, old from age rather than use, stood here and there. Though it was a warm, dry day, the shed felt damp.

He passed the fork-lift truck, which was now fussing with some hessian-wrapped bundles, and reached a raised glass office at the far end of the shed. Mrs Boseley sat here. She didn't really need the office to be raised: she seemed to be looking down on everyone already. She was about forty, with the sort of face people call handsome. This might have been expected to appeal to Duffy, but it very much didn't: he liked women small and dark and friendly, like Carol, not high-boned and aloof and eight-ninths hidden beneath the surface. Her blonde hair was scraped back off her face and pinned at the nape of her neck with an ivory comb. She examined Duffy's cards as if he had offered her an expired Libyan passport. Duffy determined to be as polite to her as he could possibly manage. He didn't find it easy.

'Worked for Mr Hendrick long, have you?' she began.

'A bit. Off and on.'

'Enjoyed it, did you?'

'All right.'

'Nice wife Mr Hendrick has.'

Duffy didn't know whether that was a question or a statement. He didn't even know if Hendrick had a wife. He decided to treat it as a statement and let it go.

'And he tells me you've done all sorts of odd jobs for him.'

'Uh-huh.'

'What sort of things?'

'This and that . . . Lifting things.' Duffy vaguely thought this must be a qualification for working here. At the same time, he felt pissed off that he was being cross-examined: Hendrick had assured him the interview would be a formality. Maybe the woman was only keeping him in here so that the others wouldn't get suspicious of him.

'Mow the lawn?'

'I beg your pardon?'

'You've mowed the lawn for Mr Hendrick, for instance?'

'Sometimes.'

Why, Mrs Boseley thought, didn't the fellow ever say yes? But Duffy never said Yes; he either nodded, or went Uh-huh, or said All right. Carol thought that you could ask Duffy to marry you and he'd half look away, nod and say, All right. This was only a guess. She had asked once, and he'd half looked away, gone quiet, and then said, 'No'.

'Well, I can't say we've exactly established your qualifications for the job, but we do want someone in a hurry, and if Mr Hendrick recommends you then I suppose that's the end of the matter.' She looked up and gazed at Duffy expressionlessly for a few seconds. He thought it was his turn to speak.

'Thank you very much, Mrs Boseley.'

'Hmm. I should say one thing to you though. The manner of your appointment is – how shall I put it – just a trifle irregular.'

'Uh-huh.' (She didn't know the half of it.)

'Normally what happens in such circumstances is that the men who work here might be expected to suggest someone: one of their friends, for instance. These are hard times, you know, and everyone knows someone who's out of a job.'

'I see.'

'I'm glad you do. Then you won't be surprised if you encounter a little, how shall I put it, a little hostility at first?'

'It doesn't bother me.'

'I hope it doesn't.' She put her head outside her glass cage and shouted at someone Duffy couldn't see.

'Tan. Tan, ask Gleeson to come up, will you?'

They sat in silence until the door opened and a muscularly plump man in a dark blue boiler suit came in; he had dark hair and mutton-chop whiskers. He looked without acknowledgement at Duffy before turning to the desk.

'Mrs Boseley?'

'Gleeson, this is Duffy, who as I told you is joining us. Make him comfortable, show him around, tell him what to do, will you?'

Gleeson nodded and left the room. Duffy glanced at Mrs Boseley but only met the top of her head as it bent over some invoices. He followed Gleeson out into the body of the cargo shed. As soon as he had caught up, Gleeson marched him across to a row of lockers and tapped the only one with a key in the door.

'Yours. Overalls. In you get.'

'I'm not that small,' said Duffy, but Gleeson declined to smile. Duffy opened the locker and saw a pair of overalls. He also saw a Page Three girl pasted inside the door and a miniature tiger dangling on a string.

'McKay's,' said Gleeson by way of explanation. The same name probably also explained why Duffy's overalls were over-generously cut.

'There's room for another in here,' he said. But Gleeson was already moving on.

'You drive a forkie?' he said suddenly.

'What?'

'You drive a forkie?' Ah, a fork-lift truck.

'I'm sure I'll pick it up.'

'Well, you can start with a trolley, or a barrer. McKay could drive a forkie. Very neat. We reckoned he could pick an apple off your head with it, like whatsisname.'

'Tell.'

'I just told.'

Gleeson walked him round the shed, pointing out various areas: Perishables, Dries, Refrigerated, and so on. Occasionally he'd introduce him: there was someone called Tan who appeared to be Chinese; someone called Casey, tall, long-haired and even surlier than Gleeson; a couple of drivers, and someone who's name Duffy forgot. Then Gleeson told him to wait around in a corner of the shed until someone asked him to do something. Like being stood in the dunce's corner, Duffy thought. Occasionally throughout the morning Gleeson gave him orders: he had to load and unload things; a couple of times he was asked to move a large packing case just a few yards, to a point which seemed no more sensible or useful than where it had started from. Duffy didn't ask; he just did it. Maybe it was some sort of initiation; maybe they were just buggering him about.

When the dinner whistle went he had just finished loading up a Transit van with Casey, who muttered what sounded like 'Canteen', and sloped off. Duffy followed and soon found himself hunched over pie and beans. Casey was eating double pie and double beans. Duffy stared at Casey's hands. The first joint of each finger of his right hand had a letter tattooed on it: H A T E was what they spelt. Always on the right hand, of course, on the fist used for persuading people. Duffy knew what he'd see on the other hand – L O V E it read – but this time there was a slight variation. The 'O' on the second finger of the hand had a sophisticated addition, a cross on the top of it: Ô. Pretty high-class tattooist, thought Duffy; wonder if he knows what it means. Casey did. As he tumbled his knife and fork on to his plate at the end of the pie and beans, he leaned across to Duffy and wiggled his second finger up and down in front of Duffy's nose.

'Courting finger,' he said, laughed, and squeaked back his chair. Two minutes later he was back, with a double sago pudding and custard. Duffy watched in silence (he felt it tactful not to be too gabby with this one) as Casey slurped it down. When he had finished putting it away he exhaled loudly.

'You courting?' he said.

'Yes,' replied Duffy straight away.

'My mistake.' But Casey's tone was still closer to belligerence than apology. 'Picked you for a wrong 'un.'

'Sorry, can't help you there,' said Duffy. He sensed that it wouldn't help him to wear a big pink star on his back around this place.

It was comforting to see Carol. For one thing, she was always so keen that it was now. She insisted by her natural mood that it wasn't the past any more, and that it wouldn't be the future until at least tomorrow. And that you didn't deserve the future until you'd made a reasonable job of the present. It was odd that she had this effect so forcefully on Duffy, because in many ways she did represent the past – the time when they were colleagues in the force, when they were going around to-gether, when they were sleeping together successfully, before Duffy was framed out of his job and his girl friend one nasty evening that he mostly tried to forget. And Carol helped him with this, refused to let him brood, insisted that he think about today, worried with him about his work. Sometimes she stayed the night, sometimes she didn't; though since he'd moved further west, out to Acton, she stayed a bit more often than when he'd been in Paddington.

They were sitting in his kitchen eating cheese on toast, and Carol was trying to stop Duffy leaping up every minute to tidy things away. Duffy was anal: there was no doubt at all about that. If he could, he'd do the washing up before the meal; Carol knew he'd secretly prefer her to hold the cheese on toast in her fingers so that he could wash up the plate. And then, when he'd done that, he'd probably hover near her with a damp J-cloth in his hand to catch any crumbs she might drop. And as for the refrigerator – it was just as bad as the last one, the one in which all the food was double-wrapped as if it were trying to escape and had to be straightjacketed; the fridge she'd called Colditz. This one, in his new flat, was no better: you opened it and saw nothing but plastic everywhere. No food, just plastic: Tup-perware boxes, plastic bags, sometimes Tupperware boxes inside plastic bags, sometimes plastic bags inside Tupperware boxes.

'What's the distinction, Duffy,' she'd once asked, 'between the things that go in polythene bags and then into Tupperware boxes, and the things that go into Tupperware boxes and then into polythene bags?'

'Ah,' he'd said. 'Ah. Now, I'm sure there's a reason. I'm positive there's a reason.' He gazed at the ceiling, trying to remember.

'Duffy,' she bellowed at him after three seconds of his reverie, 'you really think I want to know, don't you? You really think I want to know.'

'But you asked,' he replied, puzzled and mildly offended.

'Forget it. For-get. For-get. O.K.?'

'O.K.' He still couldn't work it out.

That evening he told her about Hendrick (though he didn't mention how he'd been put on to him), and about his first two days at the shed.

'Sounds like it could be a long job.'

He grunted. She felt apprehensive when he grunted. It usually meant he was about to say something she might not like.

'Can you do a couple of things?'

'I might.'

'Lend me your car in the evenings. I might need to follow someone and they'd know my van from work.'

'Maybe.'

'I mean, swop. You can have mine.'

There was a bit of a silence. Duffy had vaguely broken the rules. How would he know how to give it back at the end of the evening? Or where to give it back?

'Maybe, Duffy. But it'd have to be day-to-day. You'd have to ask each time.'

'O.K. And can you get me the traffic report on the accident this McKay had?'

'I shouldn't think so.'

'You could, though, couldn't you?'

'I might be able to get someone to read it to me. But it's not in our rules.'

'I just thought,' said Duffy quietly, 'that someone might want to do the same to me.' God he was unfair. She went and fetched her overnight bag. He knew what he'd done and felt shitty. Not about using her to get information, but about frightening her.

'Please stay.'

'No, sorry. Busy day tomorrow, beauty sleep and all that.' She ruffled his hair as if to say, It's all right really, it's just that it's not all right enough now. 'And I hope they're nicer to you at work tomorrow.'

'Oh, yes, I forgot to say – they were quite nice to me today. I mean, they weren't, as I told you, for almost all the day, and then they were.'

'Explain.'

'Well, I had to do most of the work, like yesterday, and nobody spoke to me much, and they made me do things I knew weren't necessary, and they knew I knew weren't necessary. And then at the end of the day, guess what? I looked in my locker and what did I find? Fifty quid. In very used notes.'

3

The next morning, the jumbos weren't using the M4. The whisper had got around and they were all following the North Circular. People said it was just the wind that made them land from a different direction, but Duffy knew better. Yesterday they'd obviously dug up so many divots in the runway that they were being forced to land on another one. And they wouldn't tell the passengers. That was another reason why Duffy would never fly: you never got told the truth. He'd heard enough stories from his mates to know that the first rule of any airline was, Don't scare the customers, they might yet live to come back and use us another time. So it was 'Just a little turbulence' when half the passengers could see that one of the engines was on fire; and it was 'Sorry, the captain's forgotten his Kleenex' when the hydraulics collapsed and the plane panicked back to base, jettisoning all its fuel over the Thames Estuary as it did so.

While he drove, he wondered idly about the Hendrick job. It looked like a money-earner, that was all it looked like: one of those jobs where you do your best until the client decides he's poured enough money down your drain and he'll try something else, or something better, or go to the police, or learn to live with his losses. He'd had this sort of job before. It would obviously take him some days more to work out exactly how the freight firm operated, how the terminal's security worked and how it could be bypassed; and that was just basics. He didn't know what was likely to be stolen (since in Hendrick's description it changed every time), and he didn't know who was best placed to rip it off.

So what did you do in the slow cases, the nit-picking cases, the sit-on-your-bum-and-keep-your-eyes-open cases? Well, you went back to basics, and you got the little legs working. What did he have? He had a car crash. He had a – from what he heard – badly smashed-up freight worker, whom he couldn't very well go and talk to in case he was a villain. He had a series of thefts at about monthly intervals. He had a shedful of people who weren't particularly charmed by his company – though there was no reason why they should be, if he believed Mrs Boseley, and he had no reason (apart from not liking her) not to believe her. And he had fifty quid. That was what he had most.

Cash in the locker was an old trick, of course. Everywhere in the world that there was a fiddle going – even in the place with the nice, comforting blue light outside – there was cash in the locker. For a very good reason: it sorted you out. It gave you an instant choice, and it instantly compromised you. If you handed it in, there were two problems: you might hand it in to the wrong person, someone who didn't know what was going on, someone who'd create a great stink as a consequence, and as a further consequence you might get your head rubbed up against the brickwork in some alley after work. Or you handed it in to the right person, the person who'd more or less given it to you, and then you were saying to him, 'Nice to know you're a villain; I'm not as it happens, but I do so hope we'll still get on', and then even if you were a bit bent, but just didn't want to join in this particular package scheme, this Butlins of fraud, it made you look as if you were super-clean, nothing less than old Mister White the vicar's son. And the consequence of *that* was that all the dirty jobs going somehow seemed to keep coming your way, and the sump oil just happened to get tipped down the trousers of your best suit, and the night shift fell into your lap just a bit more often than it did anyone else's, and sometimes in the canteen your arm got just a little jog as it was ladling some beans into your mouth, until finally you thought, stuff it, and you couldn't complain because you'd sound like a schoolgirl, and what had they really done to you anyway?

So, often, simply because it was easier – or because the wife wanted some new curtains, or so that you could afford a double for a change while you watched the darts match – you took it. Duffy quite understood. He didn't approve, but he didn't have any difficulty in understanding.

In the present case, he hadn't wavered for a moment. As soon as he'd seen the green bundle with the rubber band round it, he'd tucked it into the top pocket of his denim jacket. There could be someone watching, you never knew. And if there was, it was a good idea to show them a picture of instant and willing corruption.

Just to be on the safe side – there might, for all Duffy knew, have been something tiny but incriminating attached to one of the notes – he stuffed them into a brown envelope, put the date and place of finding on the outside, and gave it to Carol for safe-keeping. Now, as far as that side of things went, you just had to wait. You didn't go poling up to Gleeson, or the China-man, or whoever you guessed it to be, and say, 'Thanks very much for the money; what do I do now?' Or you didn't unless you were very stupid. You just hung around, and then after a bit, who knew how long, you'd be standing in the sun minding your own, when a voice behind you would say, 'Nice to have you with us,' and you'd turn and nod and keep your own counsel and think, so it *was* him.

But that was obviously not going to happen today, thought Duffy. Just get on with your job and keep looking around, those were the rules. He had been allotted his dunce's corner, and he was expected to sit there until they wanted him. There wasn't anything special about the corner, he realised, except that he could be watched easily, especially by Mrs Boseley in her little glass hut. Duffy trundled his trolley when asked, and found that his day consisted of the usual mix of short, back-breaking bursts of work interspersed with tedious periods of inactivity. Except that there was always something else to do. With a casual eye and a little bit of bored wandering about, he managed to work out the security system of the place. The alarm, and then on top of it the hidden trigger alarm which goes off if anyone tries to tamper with the main one: not bad, a middle-price item from about five years ago. And somewhere there'd probably be a buzzer to alert the terminal people.

At one point he wandered over to Mrs Boseley's eyrie when he noticed she wasn't there. He half-opened the door, and pretended to look inside; well, she might be under the desk or something. Then he stood politely outside the door, though the glass meant that he could see most of what he wanted to.

'Yes, what are you doing up here?' Mrs Boseley had suddenly reappeared.

'Oh, Miss, er, Mrs, I wondered if there was any work. I haven't had anything to do for a bit.'

'*I* don't give you work. Mr Gleeson gives you work.' You needed gloves to talk to her.

'Sorry, sorry. Only trying to be helpful.' And he walked cravenly back to his corner. But he'd checked the door lock, and worked out where he thought the alarm buzzer would probably be.

When the dinner whistle went, he tagged along with Casey to the canteen. It was a bit early to call it a friendship: it was more that Casey didn't actually punch Duffy's head in for following him about. They sat opposite one another while Casey consumed twice as much food as Duffy. Why didn't he get fat? Maybe he took a lot of exercise; maybe it was nothing to do with how much you ate, anyway. Duffy feared getting fat, so he didn't eat much and he took as much exercise as he could handle; he even ran up stairs sometimes – well, if he was in a hurry. Mostly, though, he just worried, and worrying about getting fat seemed to keep him thin. For the time being, anyway.

Duffy stared at Casey's long, sallow face, the thin moustache inspired by some old Charles Bronson film, the rocker-revival

48

hairdo. Was anything going on under that hairdo, he wondered. Casey never addressed him – not that Duffy minded – but as a token of incipient toleration he deigned to answer questions, as long as they weren't asked while he was eating. As he laid down his knife and fork, swabbed at the baked-bean juice on his moustache and exhaled loudly, Duffy asked him,

'You hit many people?' He indicated Casey's right hand with a deferential gesture, to fill out the inadequacy of his words. Casey looked at his hand, and as he looked it formed itself into a fist, seemingly without the authority of its owner.

'Only when I 'ave to,' he replied.

'You got any more tattoos?' Duffy asked this quickly, sensing Casey's impatience at the protractedness of their conversation.

This was one Casey could answer without words. He reached to the neck of his shirt, and pulled open the top two jeans poppers. A line of dashes ran round his throat, interspersed with letters. Duffy read:

- - - - C - U - T - - - - - H - E - R - E - - - - -

Casey's Adam's apple formed a chunky punctuation mark in this complex instruction, whose implications he allowed Duffy to take on board while he went off and fetched himself two sweets. Duffy watched him demolish them and tried to keep his mind off the idea of getting fat. He imagined a balding, middle-aged version of himself turning up to offer security assistance and being laughed away. 'We don't want a *fat* security man,' they shouted at him; 'whoever heard of a *fat* security man?'

At the end of the sweets Duffy knew he was allowed to speak again. He adopted a tone of one decidedly less brave than Casey but trying hard to put on a stiff upper lip.

'Is there – is there much violence around here?'

Casey almost smiled; that's to say, he seemed to strain a

smile through his face, and the sieved remnants of it came out the other side.

' 'ad a mate,' Casey replied, 'Big nose. Big nose.' Casey tapped the side of his own conk to help Duffy out. 'Fahnd 'im in one of them big fridges. In wif the toolips.'

Casey fell silent, looked almost reflective; then just when Duffy was about to offer his condolences, he went on loudly, with a rolling laugh:

'Didn't need to send that sod no flahs.' And he kicked Duffy hard under the table by way of emphasis.

On his way back to the shed Duffy stopped off at the telephone box and made three calls to breakers' yards in the area. Two didn't answer; they must have been out to dinner. To the third Duffy described McKay's car, and explained that his hospitalised friend had left something in it.

'Nothing like that here, mate.'

'You sure?'

'Sure I'm sure. Look, I might not be able to recognise a tiger in yer tank, but I can tell one when it's all over the cowing car, can't I?'

'Sure. Sorry, mate.'

'Any time.'

He'd have to come back to that later. Another afternoon, and then it would be Friday. Maybe he should do it this weekend – break in. He could be here for days before he picked up how the shed operated; or before he even knew the full range of stuff they transported. All he'd need was a couple of quiet hours; it wasn't as if he was going to smash anything.

But of course, he didn't need to break in. He could get Hendrick to give him the key. Assuming that Hendrick himself was on the level. Duffy never forgot about the client's angle. But if Hendrick was on the fiddle, why call in Duffy at all? Maybe there were two fiddles, one Hendrick's and one somebody else's? *It's Fiddle City, Duffy*, Willett's voice repeated in his head. Yes, but even so, Hendrick wouldn't call him in if he were on the fiddle himself, would he? Would he?

Anyway, what did it matter – if he asked Hendrick for the key, and Hendrick refused, then he threw in the job; if he asked, got it, and then something happened which made Duffy think there was more to Hendrick than he'd been told, he'd throw in the job even quicker. And then he'd take Carol out on the fifty used oncers.

Friday's work was like Thursday's, and Wednesday's and Tuesday's. When the dinner whistle blew he hopped it to the telephone box. He told Hendrick's secretary that he was still worried about the papaws. He hoped the job didn't last beyond the end of the papaw season, otherwise he'd be in trouble. She put him through.

'Mr Hendrick, it's about those papaws.' (It was always useful to remind the clients of their own pathetic security ploys; they liked that.) 'I think I might need the key.'

'The key to the papaws? Oh, you just cut them open with a knife.'

'Very amusing, Mr Hendrick.' (Very wasteful on my 10p, Mr Hendrick.) 'I'm not finding things out quick enough. I think I'd better take a look round this weekend. Can you let me have the key?'

'Er, yes, I don't see why not. But you'll have to come and collect it from my home.'

'No trouble, Mr Hendrick, it all goes on the account.' (It was also useful to remind the client of your expenses.)

Hendrick gave him an address in Fulham and asked him to call on the Saturday morning. Duffy then rang the other two breakers' yards; one of them was still out to lunch from the day before, the other, at Yiewsley, thought it might have seen the car, but couldn't remember where it was. Maybe Duffy would like to call round sometime? Yes, they were open Saturdays: until four.

So far, so good. Duffy walked quickly to the canteen where he found, to his surprise, that Casey had kept him a chair. Not that the gesture appeared to mean he was going to unbend in any other way. The same silence continued while the serious business of eating was undertaken. Except that when Casey finally thundered his sweet spoon back into his bowl, he actually addressed Duffy, for only the second time in their now burgeoning relationship.

'Where j' get the ring, then?'

'What?'

'Where j' get the ring, then, if yer not a wrong 'un?'

Ah, that; so that was what had been preying on Casey's mind all this time: the stud.

'Girl I'm courting gave it me.'

Casey in reply gave his delayed exhalation.

'Only I fort you was a wrong 'un.'

Perhaps I've made a friend, Duffy thought.

Friday afternoon was pay-day. They lined up, all six of them, at four o'clock precisely, outside Mrs Boseley's office, and went in one by one. Duffy, as the most recent recruit, was last in the queue.

'I hope my work has been satisfactory, Mrs Boseley,' he said, in a manner which he hoped might seem not too openly ingratiating. Mrs Boseley gave him one of her specially refrigerated glances, and went back to counting his wages. As she handed them over, she said,

'I wouldn't know, I haven't been watching.'

Which was only partly true, because occasionally in the last four days Duffy had looked up from his dunce's corner of the shed and noticed her blonde semi-beehive pointed in his direction. She certainly made Duffy feel watched, whether he was or not.

He went and sat on a packing case in his corner. He gazed back at the glass cubicle. Where did a woman like Mrs Boseley come from? Did she have a Christian name, for instance? Did she have a past? Did she have parents, or did she simply drop in through the roof of Hendrick's shed one day, trim and fortyish and avid to run things? She can't always have been an office manager; and she clearly didn't work her way up in Hendrick's. What could she have done before? Duffy thought of her scraped-back hair, her neat but to him unappealing figure, her bland, well-boned good looks; then he took ten, fifteen years off it, put her into a uniform (without watching while she undressed), and there she was: a stewardess. Or, as they called them then, an air hostess. That was it, that made sense. She was an ex-stewardess; they always retired them at – what was the age, he didn't know; but it was like Playboy bunnies. Rather unfair, Duffy thought; one day you're worth the free trips and the businessmen's glances, and the next it's sorry, no one wants to look at *you* any more, no there's nothing wrong, but isn't the skin round your jaw a little looser than it used to be, perhaps, and, anyway here's a nice little ground job which doesn't involve any travelling except to the loo and the canteen.

What did old stewardesses do? What did old anything do? Old golfers never die, they only lose their balls. Where had he read that? And what about old security men? What about Duffy when he got fat and old and stopped being smart any more? Would he become a nightwatchman and sit in a hut roasting chestnuts over his fire, waiting to be peed on by punks who called him Grandad? And would he perhaps be shuffling one midnight along the corridor of some factory, not because he was suspicious or anything but because he was bored and his legs needed the exercise, when some over-enthusiastic cowboy decided to take him out with the wooden end of a shotgun? It was always happening.

'Car keys.'

Duffy gave a start. Gleeson was standing next to him, chewing slightly, and making his mutton-chops shift softly up and down. Gleeson was one of those chubby people who look as if they are naturally friendly; in his case looks were deceptive.

'Your car's parked in the wrong place, can I have the keys?'

'Sorry, I'll move it.'

Duffy had his hand in his pocket and was making off when Gleeson intercepted his arm.

'Your car's parked in the wrong place.'

'Yuh, I heard.'

They stared at each other for a few seconds. Duffy found himself wondering why they'd taken all day to ask him to move it; and surely it couldn't be . . .

'Your car's parked in the wrong place.'

God he was stupid. Christ he was stupid. He wordlessly dug out his keys and handed them over. He might have hoisted it in more quickly if he hadn't been mooning over his old age, but even so . . . He felt almost ashamed of himself. You take the fifty, you wait for the connection, and then when it comes, you don't recognise it. Maybe you are getting fat, Duffy.

In a couple of minutes Gleeson returned. Duffy half expected him to say something, though he didn't quite know what; something, perhaps, like, 'Meet you behind the third frigo-container on the right.' But instead, Gleeson merely tossed the keys to Duffy from a distance of four yards and turned his back. As he caught them, Duffy looked down the shed towards Mrs Boseley's office. Did he catch a flash of blonde as a head looked away?

Well, at least something was happening. Better something than nothing, even if you don't understand it. Duffy couldn't wait for 5.30, to see why they'd wanted to move his car.

However, when the whistle blew, he loitered a bit. He changed slowly, and didn't hurry on his way to the shed door. Anyone who wanted to fall in casually beside him was more than welcome as far as Duffy was concerned. But no one did. Outside, in the small forecourt, his van was in exactly the same position as he had left it in the morning. This didn't surprise him in the least. He walked slowly across to it, waiting perhaps to be hailed by Casey, who was climbing into his Capri. But nothing happened. So Duffy eased himself into the van. Nothing on the seat. He flicked open the glove compartment: nothing there either. Nothing on the windscreen shelf. He looked over his shoulder into the back, but that all looked the same as ever. Maybe they've sawn through something in the engine, thought Duffy; but dismissed the idea as paranoid.

Then, as he was backing out of his parking space, he slipped his hand into the driver's door pocket. Polythene. Ah-hah. He lifted a package on to his crotch and didn't look at it until he was in second gear. Then he shifted his glance downwards. Calculators. Six pocket calculators; still in their boxes; still in their polythene bag.

How very kind, Duffy thought. Fifty oncers on the Wednesday, six pocket calculators on the Friday. That thought contented him for not more than half a second, then he changed up a gear into third and slowed the van until it deliberately stalled. He pulled into the side of the road, quarter of a mile from Hendrick's and half-way to the gate. Then, just in case anyone was watching, he put the van in first and turned the ignition. It fired, the van heaved forwards, and stalled again. He repeated this twice, then climbed out with a not-this-again expression, and threw up the bonnet.

He fiddled a bit with the plugs as he worked out quite why he felt unconvinced. He didn't know how these things were done, but he felt sure that they weren't done like this. You got the fifty quid, and then you got the connection; or you got the calculators and then the connection; you didn't get both and then nothing. It couldn't work like that; you had to do something to earn something. What's more, the calculators were still in their original packaging; the polythene had a couple of stickers on; even a police cadet would be able to work out where they came from.

Duffy slammed down the bonnet and climbed back into the driving seat. He took a duster and a pair of driving gloves out of the glove compartment. He pulled on the gloves, and with the duster rubbed very hard all over the polythene packing; it would be nice to leave Gleeson's dabs on it, but there was no way. Then he wrapped the package in the duster, took off the gloves, started the car, looked lengthily in the rear-view mirror, then drove off quickly. He turned sharp left, left again, right, and braked sharply in front of the Gents as if he didn't know whether or not he could hold it any longer. He ran up the path to the Gents, dived into a crapper, climbed on to the seat and tucked the calculators behind the cistern. One of these days, he thought, public crappers will go over to low cisterns like we have at home, and then where will we all be?

He smiled to himself as he drove slowly back towards the gate. He didn't mind at all being picked out at random by a security man and flagged into a special lane where a policeman was waiting. Of course he understood it was all routine. Sure, there's a lot of it about. Search away. Glove compartment, under the seats, don't miss the driver's door pocket. Brief body search, this way please, no problem, might even enjoy it he said to himself. The policeman patted him all over, and as he worked his way up the insides of his legs Duffy said to himself, Don't get too cocky. The policeman was very friendly as they went back outside to the van, where the security guard had just finished his work; he was also nice to Duffy. Duffy was nice back. He quite understood, didn't mind at all, any time, feel free, see you again soon.

As he drove off, Duffy remembered Willett and said to himself: random nose, or scientific nose? Or a bit of help?

Hendrick opened the door to Duffy with a preoccupied expression. He walked him silently down the hall and into the kitchen, scattering before him a pair of small daughters whom he instructed to go and play outside. As the back door banged, Hendrick fretted over whether he ought after all to let Duffy have the key to the freight shed. Duffy knew the situation well: first you employ someone to help you on the security side, and you tell him all your troubles, and then you start wishing you hadn't. It was a familiar psychological pattern. And there was an equally familiar way round it. You didn't stand on your dignity and get petulant and thrust your credentials down the client's throat; you just went quiet for a moment to show him you weren't as put out as he expected you to be, and then you tickled the businessman in him.

'Just as you wish, Mr Hendrick, I mean, it's really up to you.

I can't swear to you I'll find anything of use if you lend me the key. It's just that, given the sort of job this is, it'll definitely cut down the bill if I can get round the shed when there's no one there. But it's entirely up to you, of course.'

It was almost criminal the way this always worked, Duffy thought. Hendrick crumbled, apologised, agreed, dug out the key and handed it over.

'Two things, though, Mr Duffy.' This bit was familiar as well; it sprang from the need to reassert oneself as the employer, as the layer-down of conditions, the paymaster. 'First, I want to know precisely when you're going over there, and how long you'll be. And second, I want the key back as soon as you've finished with it.'

'No problem.' Duffy was deferential, as the pattern called for. 'I'm a bit tied up today, so I reckon I'll go round Sunday afternoon – middle of the afternoon; three o'clock, shall we say? I'll only be an hour or two. Can't be more exact, I'm sure you understand why' (appeal to ally, to fellow-conspirator; Hendrick duly nodded) 'and then I'll be able to give you the key back by about six, I should say. I'll stick it through your door if you're not in.'

Hendrick began to explain in unnecessary detail how to stop the alarm system being triggered when you opened the side door. Duffy half listened to this, just in case it contained anything new, and pretended to concentrate by gazing out of the kitchen window into the back garden. There was a nice crazy-paving patio outside the back door, then a bed of geraniums, then a kids' play area. There was a sandpit and a paddling pool and a slide. The two girls, who seemed about seven or eight to Duffy, were noisily playing on the slide. One of them was standing up on the top of it now. Duffy winced: it wasn't far to fall for an adult, but for a child? On to the concrete? It worried Duffy. He shifted his gaze to the brick wall at the end of the garden, which was only about a dozen yards from where he was standing, and found that there was another worry in his head, one he couldn't identify, one which had something to do

57

with the last few days but which he couldn't pin down. Meanwhile, Hendrick came to the end of his instructions about the alarm system, and Duffy nodded as if, with some difficulty, he'd just about managed to understand. Clients liked that. It made them think they had a secure system.

The first thing Duffy did as he drove west was to call at a locksmith's and get a duplicate key made. He didn't want to rely on Hendrick's vacillating assessment of his reliability if he wanted to make another visit; and besides, it was a bit of a traipse over to Fulham.

He'd lied to Hendrick about the timing of his visit to the shed. Just in case Hendrick wasn't entirely level with him, he'd decided to go at once. He reached the shed at 11.30 and opened the side door with the key he had just had made (best to check it, in case he had to take it back for refiling). The alarm worked on a trigger-delay of twenty seconds: enough time for Hendrick to toddle up a half flight of stairs and flick the cancel lever.

Duffy began by the big double doors at the southern edge of the shed. The floor was marked out with coloured lines like an indoor sports arena, and the goods were stacked on their rust-painted racks within differently sized squares and rectangles. Some areas were set aside for regular customers, and had their names on placards hanging above them: Fraser Matthews, Bamco, Holdsworth & French, and so on. Regular shipments thus went to exactly the same place in the shed week after week, month after month, making things easier for Hendrick's men – or the customers themselves, if they were collecting.

Duffy examined the freight more carefully than he was able to in the daytime, but didn't learn much. The documentation tags on the goods were informative to the person with the right to know, and deliberately uninformative to anyone else – like himself. Carrier, weight, number of packages, airway bill number, destination (which meant airport, rather than importer or recipient). Well, that was fair, if unhelpful, enough. Name, rank and number: especially number. Some of the cases announced what was inside them. Calculators here (that was a mistake – Duffy could see signs of interference with one of the cartons), American weekly journals there, refrigerated fish down the far end. Packing-cases, tea-chests, compressed-cardboard boxes, hessian-wrapped bundles. Hendrick was right – what the hell did Duffy think he was going to find just by wandering around? Did he think he was like Alice in Wonderland with her Eat-Me cakes and Drink-Me drinks: that he'd find a big packing case marked Steal Me, and all he'd have to do would be to climb into it, wait for someone to pick it up, then leap out with a pair of handcuffs dangling from his belt and shout 'Freeze'. Is that what he thought it would be like?

Still, if this bit was disappointing, he could move on to the next bit. He passed his dunce's corner and strolled over to the lockers. There were six people working there and a bank of ten lockers. With a small knife he opened the ones he'd seen his fellow employees going to: each contained a set of overalls, plus extra male appurtenances which were either useful at work or couldn't be taken home: fags, chewing gum, booze, the occasional dirty mag, greasy sweaters. Casey's locker contained a bottle of Listerine mouthwash, which took Duffy aback; perhaps there was a secret Casey he didn't know about, one who combed cologne into his hair and shaved his armpits?

Duffy then opened the four lockers which he'd never seen anyone use. Two were empty; one contained a copy of the *Sun* from two years ago, the other an unopened tin of dog food. Duffy closed them all carefully, and moved off. Then he had a hunch. He walked back and opened his own locker and looked inside. Hmmm. He nodded to himself. Exactly as he had left it yesterday. So much for hunches.

The lock on Mrs Boseley's door detained him for about a minute and a half. Again, he had to move quickly to the cancel lever on the alarm. Then, having checked the precise location of the alarm buzzer under the desk, he sat down in her chair and surveyed the shed from Mrs Boseley's angle. Yes, there was no doubt you could see a lot better from up here, even if it was only about four feet above the level of the rest of the shed. Over there was that turd Duffy's corner; that was where we made the little bugger stand; that was where we made him push his trolley and eat shit. Have some calculators, Mr Duffy. Don't forget to declare them at the gate, Mr Duffy. Few weeks in prison do you, Mr Duffy?

He stopped himself. He didn't like Mrs Boseley, but he had no reason to believe that she had anything to do with the calculators. The fact that he wanted her to meant that he ought to be doubly careful before concluding that she did. Stop hating her, Duffy. Go through her desk instead.

He took out a notebook and started slowly working his way through the desk. He went through box-files full of invoices and copied down the names and telephone numbers of what seemed to be the regular clients. Business looked pretty healthy, as far as Duffy could judge, though he had to admit he wouldn't recognise a book-keeping fiddle if it stood up and played a tune for him.

Then he went through the recent correspondence and saw why Hendrick had decided to employ him. One wholesaler of furs had decided to take his business elsewhere – it wasn't that he wasn't insured, it was just that if it happened once, it might happen twice, Mr Hendrick, mightn't it, and it's so inconvenient (nothing personal, of course) – and a general dealer had said how seriously unhappy he was about the loss of a case of Italian sunglasses.

In the top left-hand drawer he found Mrs Boseley's dressing-table: powders, lotions, creams, lipsticks, combs, mirrors; if he looked hard enough, he'd probably find the collar-stiffeners she put inside her cheeks before talking to him. Instead, he went on to the next drawer, where he found her address book. This detained him for some time, though with little profit: no names which made him jump out of her chair; many of the regular clients' numbers, which was hardly surprising. He looked up the addresses and phone numbers of all Hendrick Freight's employees, and copied them down. He rechecked B for Boseley, but she appeared to know no one else of her own name. He flipped to the fly-leaf and copied down the home address and telephone number of Mrs E. Boseley. That 'E' was the only thing about her he'd found out so far. E for Eskimo.

He carried on through the drawers and encountered only the normal paraphernalia of office life – a stapler that had conked out, some perished rubber bands, the unused packet of Pritt Buddies. In the third drawer down on the right-hand side, however, he found something which was clearly peculiar to this office: a photograph in a frame, placed face-down in the drawer. Duffy very slowly turned it over, as a magician turns over his predictably surprising card. As he did so, he vibrated his tongue against his palate to make a quiet drum-roll noise, then went 'Ta-taaaaaa TUM' as the face turned the right way up.

It was no one he knew. The photo showed a round-faced man in his forties; balding, with little round gold-rimmed glasses, and an indulgent smile on his lips; he was wearing a chalk-striped suit with a rather elaborate buttonhole. A wedding photograph, perhaps? Mr Boseley? Was there a Mr Boseley? It was a recent photo; had the office manager got married in the last five years? He didn't know. The most probable solution was, of course, the simplest: that it *was* Mr Boseley, and the fact that Duffy wanted it not to be – wanted, indeed, for it to be some brutish lover with a fully equipped torture dungeon – made him wary of going along with this fancy. One slight question lingered in his mind. It was understandable that you didn't want to put such a photo on your desktop – people would only smirk at it and Mrs Boseley didn't look the sort who cared for smirks, but if you put it in a drawer, so that you could reach down and take a look whenever you felt glum, or beset, or sexy, or curse-ridden, wouldn't you put it in face upwards?

Duffy reset the alarms as he left and drove to the breakers' yard. He'd rung them about this mate's car, the customised Cortina. Not me you talked to, squire. Cortina, eh? Painted to look like a tiger? Well, I'd remember *that*, wouldn't I? Think you're out of luck, squire. Well, all right, if you insist. Into the hut, check the books. Yes, we had *a* Cortina, but it's about this size now (gesture like a fantasising fisherman). Amazing how small these crushers can get things, isn't it? You sure it was sent on here?

Still, it was a bit of a long shot anyway. And by seven o'clock it didn't matter. Carol rang.

'Sorry, I tried to get you yesterday, but you seemed to be out.'

'. . .'

'It's about that car.'

'Good.'

'I had the report read to me. As far as they could work out there must have been some sort of collision before it went over the barrier. There was paint on the offside rear wing from another vehicle, and quite a severe dent in the side where the point of impact was.'

'Puncture?'

'They said the tyres were fine.'

'Steering?'

'They said the car was in good nick. Apart from being crashed, of course.'

'And nothing on the other vehicle.'

'Not a thing. No one stopped. No one saw anything.'

'That's a great help, love. Thank you.' Carol smiled at the telephone. You didn't get those two words out of Duffy very often. She mused fondly on him.

But Duffy was musing elsewhere. He was thinking: what do you kill for – as near as makes no difference? Do you kill for a case of Italian sunglasses? Do you kill for a couple of boxes of smoked salmon?

4

'Right on time, Mr Hendrick.' It was always a good idea to point out your own virtue to clients.

'Ah, yes, thank you, Duffy.' Hendrick stood on his front door step and held his hand out for the key. He didn't look particularly pleased to see Duffy.

'Wondered if I could have a quick word, actually.'

'Hmm? Oh, very well.' He led Duffy down the hall and into the kitchen, gloomily shooing the children into the garden yet again. This time they seemed more reluctant than last time. Maybe they got shooed into the garden too much for their own liking. And was there a Mrs Hendrick around?

'Suppose I should have asked you before, Mr Hendrick, but do you mind if we run through your employees? Fill me in on them?'

'Fine, go ahead.'

'Mr Gleeson.'

'You don't suspect Mr Gleeson?' Hendrick looked across at Duffy as if he'd got Gleeson handcuffed to him already, gold bars pulling his pockets out of shape and diamonds dripping out of his turn-ups.

'I don't suspect anyone, Mr Hendrick, anyone in particular yet. But if you don't start by suspecting everyone then you start suspecting no one, and then you don't see anything.' It wasn't really true, any of this, but it was the formula the clients seemed to like; it made them feel all right about telling dirt on their favourite employees. And Duffy had deliberately started with someone whom Hendrick probably trusted, so that they wouldn't have to go through the argument again when it came to Mrs Boseley. 'There are certain routines of investigation which may strike you as irritating, but I'm afraid if you want a professional job done they have to be gone through.' They liked that line too: it appealed to a shared professionalism, as well as to the small boy in them.

'Of course, of course. Well, Gleeson's a splendid chap. Been with me four years. Hard-working, never missed a day, gets on with the others.'

'Tan – Chinese, is he?'

'No, Malaysian, I think. Well, he's very oriental, isn't he? Yellow and doesn't say much.'

'Maybe that's because he doesn't speak the language too well.'

'Oh, he does, born and brought up here. Nice chap, works hard. Very strong. Does that thing with his hands they all do out there . . .'

'Origami?' (Careful, Duffy, he thought to himself, don't get too smartass; but Hendrick didn't blink.)

'No, that smashing bricks and things with the side of your hand.'

'Oh yes, I know what you mean.' Well, thanks for the warning.

'Casey?'

'Nice chap,' (oh, *come on*, Mr Hendrick) 'works hard. Bit slow on the uptake sometimes. Good driver.'

Duffy asked about the other two – Botsford and McAndrew – then, slightly apprehensively,

'And, you know, just as a matter of pure routine – Mrs Boseley?'

Hendrick looked at him sharply, and Duffy gave him the we've-talked-about-it gesture.

'Oh yes, very well. Splendid lady, very efficient, completely trustworthy, never misses a day, gets on with the employees very well.'

64

And runs a wolf-cub pack in the evening, no doubt, under the name of Akela or something. Hendrick was useless. He obviously had a group of model employees – clean, hardworking, honest, healthy, and so on. It was just that one of them was nicking his stuff, that was all. Duffy switched his tone, as if the professional side of the talk were over, and they were now man-to-man over a couple of beers.

'I'm bound to agree with you, Mr Hendrick, she's a terrific lady. I certainly knew where I was right from the beginning. She been with you since you started up?'

'Oh yes, five years Mrs Boseley's been with us.'

'What did she do before? Just out of interest. I was wondering what that sort of lady would have done before.'

'I think she was a senior stewardess on one of the big airlines.' Hendrick spoke with the tone of one saying less than he knew.

'Why didn't she stay on? She could be running B.A. by now, couldn't she?'

'Well *I* think she could, naturally, but I suppose she thought that if she couldn't do what she wanted to do, it was best to get out. They don't let them go on being hostesses after a certain time, you know. Silly rule.'

'I agree. I suppose . . . ' Duffy's tone became even more bottom-of-the-glass, 'I suppose there's a Mr Boseley?'

Hendrick laughed, which was a rare occurrence, and his corpse's suit juddered about at the unexpected upheaval within it. A dirty lock of blond hair fell across his face.

'Now I see where you're leading, Mr Duffy. I'm afraid the answer is, I don't fancy your chances.'

Duffy persuaded his voice to join in the laugh. 'Oh, it wasn't for myself I was asking. I just thought, you know, pity such a splendid lady has to earn her own living.'

Hendrick still looked roguish, still clearly disbelieved him. 'Well I gather there is one, but I think he's an invalid. One doesn't like to pry, but they do say he's in an iron lung. Poor Mrs Boseley.'

Poor *Mr* Boseley, thought Duffy; not only in an iron lung, but having Mrs B. as your ray of sunshine. He shifted his tone back to the professional one.

'What about McKay? What was he like?'

'Oh, very hard worker, good driver, been with us some years.' Helped run Mrs Boseley's wolf-cub pack, no doubt. Very handy with a tent-peg. Drove old ladies across the street in his tiger car. Did a lot of work for charity.

'So what we have, Mr Hendrick, is that all your employees have been with you for some time – at least a couple of years?'

'Yes.'

'And thefts only started about six months ago.'

'Yes.'

'Hmm. And one other thing. I suppose none of your employees have criminal records?'

Hendrick pushed the dirty blond lock back where it belonged.

'Oh, but I'm sure they're perfectly rehabilitated.' Uh-huh.

'Tell me, Mr Hendrick.' Duffy was getting extremely pissed off, but tried to sound merely reproachful.

'Well, Tan did knife someone once; but he was very young, he didn't know what he was doing. I'm sure it was under extreme provocation. That's why he's taught himself to do that thing with his hands.' (So that he breaks their bones instead of having to knife them.) 'And Casey has hit a few people in his time.'

'How many convictions?'

'Four, actually. But it was always a six-and-two-threes situation, from what he tells me. I mean, I don't think he'd hit anyone just for the pleasure of hitting them.'

'Don't you think I ought to have known this before?' Bloody clients.

'Oh, well, I didn't think it was relevant. I mean, none of my employees have any convictions for stealing. And none of them have got into fights – not on my premises anyway. I'm afraid I thought it might only prejudice you if I told you earlier.'

'All I can say is, Mr Hendrick, you're a very fair-minded man.' And a fucking fool.

He supposed he believed Hendrick. He thought he was pretty wet and pretty naïve; but he supposed he believed him. In a funny way, too, Duffy almost agreed with him. The public always thought, once a criminal, always a criminal; they also thought that once you've committed one crime, then it's as if you're in a great supermarket – you just pick any crime you fancy off the shelf. Duffy knew it didn't work like that. Some crimes go with other crimes, some don't. White-collar criminals, for instance: they usually stuck with white-collar crime (who wouldn't, it was so lucrative). And arsonists, they were really odd buggers. Just liked committing arson, all the time; nothing but arson. Have a house burnt out and it's no good rounding up the cosh men and the bank robbers; you have to find a nut with a box of matches, someone who used to like watching the fire engines go by as a kid, someone who's probably quite timid and entirely law-abiding – except that he likes burning people to death.

So, theft and assault? Well, there was a much closer connection there. But not a necessary connection. Sometimes you hit people to steal from them; sometimes you stole and then had to hit people to get away. But an awful lot of people liked hitting other people just for itself. They liked it. It made them feel good. And it stopped the person they hit from carrying on irritating them. Duffy understood that. If you were a Malaysian brought up over here, didn't feel particularly Malaysian, just bloody looked it all the time, you'd get fed up after a few years of school with all the kids pulling slit eyes at you and talking in sing-song voices and aiming kung-fu kicks at you which might just occasionally land, and most of all pointing out all the time that there were more of them than there were of you, and that's how it was always going to be, and that's a nice biro, Chinky-

Winky, I fink I'll have that. Wouldn't you fancy carving a few stitches into someone after a bit of that? And if you did, and had, it wouldn't necessarily make you want to start nicking Italian sunglasses ten years later, would it?

Hmmm. Duffy could see the Hendrick view, but at the same time it was a bit wet-panted, a bit sentimental. You could just as well argue the line that, if Tan knifed someone at school, then afterwards the kids would probably have treated him differently. Don't tangle with the crazy Chink killer: the eye-pulling and the kung-fu kicks would have fallen off. Kids respect violence and madness – not wet, introverted madness, of course, but crazy, outgoing, killer-madness. No doubt Tan got an easier ride at school after the knife episode. And no doubt he could have concluded that crime, in its funny way, does pay. That would be just as logical, wouldn't it? And the logic would continue with the idea: it pays even more if you don't get caught. Duffy knew from experience how to read a criminal record. He did it as policemen always do: reading any acquittals as convictions, doubling up the number of convictions, seeing the guilty pleas for what they probably were – a way of getting off a heavier charge – and filling in between the recorded convictions all manner of other, undetected crimes.

Duffy was letting his mind freewheel because of an acute shortage of facts. All he could do was play about with the few he had. He wouldn't have minded a bedside chat to McKay, but that was far too risky; too many possible connections. Instead, he rang Carol and asked her to run half a dozen names through the computer. He wanted to check the record against what Hendrick had given him. As an afterthought he added another name – Hendrick's. You never can tell.

Carol didn't want to do it. She didn't like the way Duffy just used her as part of the service he offered clients. It was also strictly against police regulations. She could be fired on the spot. Duffy exaggerated the importance of the check, and she finally agreed. It wouldn't, after all, be that risky; and he did need it for his work; and he was, really, in the same line of business as her.

He also asked if she would lend him her car that evening; but she refused. He could have it the following evening, but not tonight. Duffy agreed, rang off, and imagined her down at the roller-disco with John Travolta, who was excuse-me'd in mid-shuffle by Robert Redford, who squired her off to an operatically candlelit dinner (why was she still wearing her uniform in his fantasy?) and then, later, back at his place, made her weep and croon with joy and delight. Meanwhile, Carol was thinking: well, I *could* have put off Auntie this one time, but you've got to have some principles with men; especially with Duffy.

At work, on the Monday, there was a tricky thing to be done. Gleeson. Duffy hoped he wouldn't balls it up. It was a question of getting the right manner as much as anything. It was also a question of not bringing it up too soon, so that they had a little sweat about what might have happened; but also not leaving it too long, so that they thought nothing at all had happened. Duffy spent some of the day wondering whether Malaysians needed sunglasses in the English climate; and then, about mid-afternoon, he thought he'd better do it now before he'd thought about it too many times. He spotted Gleeson, clipboard in hand, checking some cases and wandered casually over to him.

'Can you give me a hand with my car?'

Gleeson didn't look up, and went on checking his list.

'It's parked in the wrong place.'

Gleeson ignored him.

'It's parked in the wrong place.'

Still Gleeson ignored him. He pursed his lips over the clipboard and the mutton-chops shifted forwards.

'It's parked in the wrong place.'

'Fuck off, Duffy,' said Gleeson in a quiet, seemingly friendly tone.

If you couldn't get him to come outside, you'd have to say it here. Or you could try something different, to stop him telling you to fuck off. In almost an undertone Duffy said,

'I take it you were wearing gloves, Gleeson, because I certainly was.'

Then he wandered slowly away, out through the double doors and round to the car park. A minute later they were standing side by side peering into the engine of Duffy's van. Gleeson's mere presence told Duffy something extra: that he hadn't been wearing gloves.

'Now, what about Friday?'

'What about Friday?'

'The stuff in my car.'

'What stuff?'

'The calculators.'

'What calculators?' Christ, it was like an English lesson for foreign students; repeat everything I say but turn it into a question.

'There were calculators in my car on Friday.'

'You been nicking calculators, mate? Better watch I don't report you.'

'You put six calculators in my car on Friday.'

'Now why would I do a thing like that? 'Snot your cowing birthday or anything is it?'

'And quite by chance I was stopped by a random check at the gate.'

'Very good, the security round here. Tight as oats.'

'You borrowed my car keys on Friday.'

'Did I, mate? Expect I wanted to move your car or something.'

'You didn't move my car.'

'Then why would I want to borrow your keys? Be logical, mate.'

Duffy felt he wasn't quite on top of the argument. 'Why did you come out here as soon as I mentioned wearing gloves?'

'Is that what you were saying? I could hear you muttering something. I thought you wanted a hand with your car. That's why I came out. Now you start telling me you've been nicking calculators. I think maybe this job's getting too much for you, Duffy.' Gleeson smiled in a friendly way; he knew how to look friendly as long as he didn't mean it. The only thing to do was to change course.

'O.K., let's start the conversation again. Let's pretend the car's fixed. Let's pretend you moved it on Friday. Let's pretend I don't somewhere have a package which might or might not have someone's fingerprints on it.' (Not that that would prove anything, Duffy realised.) 'Let's pretend I wasn't given a shakedown at the gate on Friday, and that in any case if I was, it was completely random. O.K.?'

'I think this job's getting too much for you.' Duffy kept doggedly on.

'So we're starting now instead. I need this job, Gleeson. I don't like it any more than any other job, but I need it. It's not a good time not to have a job. Now, I don't mind the fact that you give me shitty things to do, and make me move packing cases which you and I know fucking well don't have to be moved. I don't mind the fact that you give me a shitty corner of the shed to stand around in. I don't want to join in your card games because I don't play cards. I don't even care why you don't want me to work here; that's your business. All I'm telling you is I'm working here, and I'm fucking going on working here, and you can bleeding well get used to it. And if you try and fuck me around, then I'll fucking fuck you around, I can promise you that.'

Duffy hoped the way he veered from pathos to aggression, and then to manic insistence, would have some effect. The trouble was, he didn't really have any threats in his locker. 'Or I'll let your tyres down . . . ' 'Or I'll stamp on your shoe-laces . . . ' – that was what it sounded like to him. He just hoped it sounded more convincing to Gleeson; he hoped the existence and current location of the calculators might give him just a little leverage. All he could do would be to hang on, keep his head down and watch out for people trying to fuck him up.

At least Gleeson was looking serious as they walked back to the shed. His bushy eyebrows were pushing together in thought. As they came through the double doors he turned confidentially to Duffy.

'By the way, I shouldn't nick any more of them calculators, Duffy. I mean, you can't work more than one at a time, can you?'

As Duffy got on with his work he reflected that this conversation, necessary as it had been, would also have the unwanted effect of freezing things. Gleeson (assuming that it was just Gleeson, or 'they' if there were a 'they') would know that Duffy would be on the lookout for being fucked up, for having a dead cat stuffed up his exhaust pipe, or whatever. He'd be watching them (assuming 'them'), and they'd be watching him. They might try and fuck him up; they'd most probably just leave him alone in his dunce's corner; what they certainly wouldn't do would be to follow up the fifty quid in the locker (assuming, of course, that this is what the money was about in the first place; on the other hand, maybe it was just a bit of preliminary bait so that he'd accept the calculators). Whichever way, Duffy realised that he was going to be hard pushed to get a break from this end of things. He'd just have to see if his out-of-hours legwork turned up anything.

So began an extremely boring fortnight for Duffy. Every other day he phoned the third breakers' yard, but they never replied. He borrowed Carol's rusting Mini on the nights it was available, and each evening tailed one of four people; Gleeson, Tan, Casey and Mrs Boseley. That's to say, he drove his van round to Carol's, picked up the Mini, drove to one of the addresses he'd listed in his notebook, and sat around waiting for something to happen. It wasn't much good as a technique for getting to know their routines; it was, in fact, only just marginally more useful than staying at home and pulling his wire; but at least he felt, as his bum grew more numb by the hour, as if he was more or less earning his money.

The flaw in the schedule, of course, was that by the time he got into position outside where they lived, they'd often gone out for the evening already. Casey, for instance, seemed to turn round after work in just a few minutes – a quick rinse with Listerine was probably his idea of slipping into something loose. Two evenings were spent fruitlessly outside Casey's squat in Heston before Duffy realised that he had already gone out and was probably exercising his specially tattooed courting finger in some cinema car park. The third evening Duffy took a risk and followed him straight from work in his van. That evening, of course, Casey decided to stay in. The next day he asked Duffy over double pie and beans,

'Seeya figh' last nigh'?'

Duffy regretted that he hadn't; Casey assured him it had been a figh' inna million.

With Gleeson he had to sit outside a large semi in Uxbridge; there was a Mrs Gleeson and, by the sound of it, a baby Gleeson. Maybe this explained why they didn't go out much. At least, they didn't go out on the nights Duffy chose. The only thing that slightly surprised him was the two cars shunted up against each other on the small concrete parking space: the Viva which Gleeson came to work in, and a big Granada, V-registration. Maybe Mrs Gleeson had private means.

Tan was a bit more interesting. He lived with his family on the edge of Southall. He went out most evenings with his girl-friend – though, fortunately for Duffy, not before he'd had a good Malaysian meal with his parents first. Duffy imagined this meal while munching a pork pie and driving as fast as he could from Carol's flat back to Southall. If he hurried he'd get there in time to follow Tan taking his girl friend to a cinema, or to the pub, or once, for a walk in the park.

Mrs Boseley lived in Rayners Lane, which was marginally more convenient for Duffy – out along the Western Avenue and then cut through. She seemed to like watering her front garden in the evenings, which meant that Duffy had to park some way off. The other thing she seemed to enjoy was having friendly chats with her neighbours. It didn't seem very much to report back to Hendrick about.

This routine was heavy on petrol. It was also heavy on Duffy's patience. Nine nights of it on the trot and he couldn't stand any more. He gave himself the evening off and went down the Gemini Club. This was where he trawled when the Alligator was feeling a bit stale, when he was tired of the same old faces sipping vermouth, when he wanted a bit more of the unexpected, a bit more of the chase. It wasn't rough at the Gemini, but it was a bit more competitive. You had to work for your trade down there, spend a bit more; but the merchandise was a lot more varied. Duffy had a very nice Swede snaffled from under his nose (it was a members' club, but foreigners were allowed in on presentation of their passports); he got home eventually with a shy publishing trainee who flirted quite hard, got Duffy to buy him too many drinks, told him in the van that he'd never done anything like this before (Duffy didn't believe him, but assured him it wouldn't hurt), and then got scratchy about leaving his watch in the Tupperware box. He walked around the flat, naked and drunk, with his watch still on, exclaiming, 'But I want to time us, I want to time us.' Eventually, when Duffy expressed impatience, the guy pulled a long face, trudged obediently to the bathroom, dropped his watch in the box and was promptly sick into it as well. As Duffy was rinsing the sick off the watch and listening to the snores from the settee, he vowed his loyalty to the Alligator once more.

The next night but one something happened. Mrs Boseley went to town. At 8.30 she came out of her front door and gave Duffy a shock. She didn't have a watering can in her hand; she didn't look around for a neighbour to chat to; she walked straight to her car and drove off. What's more, she had put her hair down.

She was a confident driver, but he followed her without much difficulty into the West End. She clearly knew her way around; Duffy knew his even better. Three years as a detective-sergeant in Soho and he still remembered every alleyway, every one-way street, and most of the possible crimes. Mrs Boseley parked in Great Marlborough Street; he drove past her, stopped thirty yards on, and watched in his wing mirror as she got out and locked the car. He tailed her down Poland Street, along Broadwick Street, a left and a right, and then she suddenly disappeared into a club. He stood around some twenty yards short of the entrance for a few minutes, then crossed the street and strolled slowly along the pavement on the other side.

Dude's, it was called, and even from across the street it didn't look the sort of place which Mrs Boseley would know about – not the Mrs Boseley he'd met anyway. There was a maroon awning over the entrance with 'Dude's' written on it in three-foot-high copper-plate handwriting. There were velvet curtains in the windows, held back with lace ties; but though the curtains were drawn back, you couldn't see through the window because there were shutters as well on the inside, and these were closed. To work out what it might be like you had to consult the large display cases on either side of the entrance, which contained big colour transparencies lit from behind.

Duffy crossed the road and quickly took them in. There was a picture of a curving bar with lots of stools, none of them occupied; there was a picture of what might have been a dining area, showing various booths with waist-high slatted swing doors. There were also two pictures of very pretty girls, one dark and one blonde, each with bare shoulders. At the top of the display box on the left Duffy read: 'DUDE'S – WHERE GENTLEMEN RELAX'; at the top of the right-hand box he read: 'DUDE'S – FOR THE BEST IN COMPANY'.

He walked on, and took up a station some thirty yards beyond the club entrance. After about an hour Mrs Boseley emerged, and without a glance began to walk swiftly back towards her car. Duffy tailed her for long enough to guess with safety that she was going home; then he turned off, drove the Mini back to Carol's place and swapped cars. He pushed the keys through the door; Carol had insisted on that. As he drove off, Duffy stared balefully at the cars parked near by. Wasn't that one Paul Newman's?

At work the next day he found himself occasionally looking down the shed to Mrs Boseley's glass eyrie. Well, well, well, he thought. The regular, reliable job, the little house in Rayners Lane, the watering can, the husband in the iron lung – and suddenly, hair down and off to the tacky club. What did it mean; what *did* it mean? Was she turning the odd trick on the side to help with her husband's medical expenses? If so, would it be worth it, driving all the way into town for just an hour? You'd have to do something incredibly filthy to make it worth your while, Duffy thought. And when she came out, she didn't look as if she'd just done something incredibly filthy.

Maybe there was an entirely innocent explanation. There never was, in Duffy's experience; but try. Maybe her brother worked there; or something like an illegitimate daughter. Did you visit your illegitimate daughter at work? And why did she put her hair down? She looked, Duffy had to admit it, better with her hair down, less frosty. Almost like someone who wasn't nasty.

The enigma kept Duffy happy all day. What's more, he knew that tonight it wasn't going to be following Tan to the Malaysian disco in Hayes, thank you very much. After work he rang Carol to check if he could call by; no, he didn't need her car. What he did need was the brown envelope he'd left with her. He didn't reckon that Gentlemen Relaxed for peanuts. He also reckoned that they didn't relax in green suede blousons with big plastic zips up the front and polo-neck sweaters and jeans. Part of Duffy thought, Stuff it, I'm paying, why shouldn't I dress as I please? The more sensible part thought, don't stand out any more than you have to. He dug into the very back of his wardrobe and came up with a real copper's suit, a delicate mud colour with tight trouser-bottoms and lapels as narrow as the triangles on a backgammon board. He pulled it on and didn't like the feeling around his waist; he undid the two elasticated button-fastenings at the sides, but that didn't seem to make any difference. Just filling out with maturity, he said to himself; but the other voice whispered, Getting fat, Duffy, getting *fat*.

He found a tie as thin as a runner bean and pulled it round his neck. As he was doing it up he felt like a suicide; Christ, fat *neck* too. Then he examined himself in the mirror. He looked ridiculous. He looked like a member of a 1960s band which had modelled itself on Gerry and the Pacemakers and got nowhere; he twiddled some drumsticks to himself. The last thing he looked like was a Gentleman about to Relax. Should he take the stud out of his ear? Should he change his desert boots? Hell, no – he'd compromised enough already. Wait till they saw the colour of his extremely used one-pound notes: then they'd know who they were dealing with.

When Carol saw him she burst out laughing.

'Where you going, Duffy? Revival disco?'

'That bad, is it? I thought I looked quite smart.'

'Duffy, you look chronic.' And she kissed him on the lips in sheer delight at how awful he looked. His waistband was cutting into him and made him want to pee. When he returned, Carol said,

'Oh, I checked out those names for you. Sorry it took so long, but I didn't want to take any risks.'

'Sure. Thanks, love. What did you find?'

She handed him a piece of paper. He read it quickly. Exactly as Hendrick had said. And Hendrick himself was clean. Still, he'd better be grateful.

'That's very useful, love. That's just what I needed.'

'How's it going?' She hadn't asked any more what 'it' was, because she didn't really want to know. But she worried about Duffy's career in a general way.

'Not very well. Slow job. Still, it's paying.'

'That's the main thing.' She went and fetched his brown envelope. He took out the money and stuffed it in his pocket. As he left the flat – Carol was suppressing a giggle at the sight of his flat-cut jacket bottom, like something out of an old gangster film – he began to feel like a man of means. He could very well pass for a Gentleman, in the dark with the light behind him.

He parked in Great Marlborough Street and walked away from the car with a pair of flapping hands inside his stomach. He made his way down to Dude's, which was new since he had left the patch. What would it be like? Would it be posh? Would it be dirty? Whatever it was, it would beat sitting in a rusty Mini at Rayners Lane.

The double glass doors said Dude's on them. The custom-built doormat said Dude's on it. The inner double glass doors said Dude's on them. They were certainly good at letting you know where you were. Inside, it seemed very dark to Duffy at first. On his left was a cloakroom opening with a girl standing in it. He might have stopped anyway, but he definitely stopped now. Her breasts were completely bare, and very nice too, he thought.

'Your hat, sir,' she said.

'I don't have a hat.'

'No; your hat, sir.'

He moved closer towards her. Was he being very stupid? Was it O.K. to look at her breasts?

'I'm sorry,' he said, 'this is my first time here.'

'That's quite all right, sir,' she replied with a toothpaste smile. 'You will be taking one of the girls downstairs, of course.'

'Oh, of course.'

'Twenty pounds, please, sir.'

'Oh, of course.'

He slowly counted out two-fifths of his bundle and wondered what he was paying for. Wondered who he was paying for as much as anything. Where was downstairs? And where were the girls?

He needn't have worried. As he turned away from the hat-check girl he saw them. To his right was the long curved bar

pictured outside, though it seemed smaller and less luxuri-
ously appointed than in its photograph. There were about
fifteen girls variously clustered round the bar, five or so of
them attending to a fat man at the far end. There were, he
noticed, many different types of girl here, including a token
black girl and a token Chinese (or perhaps a token Malaysian),
but they all had one thing in common: their breasts were bare.
Except for one, that is, who wore a leotard. As Duffy walked
across towards the bar this girl mechanically lowered the top of
her leotard so that he could see her breasts; they swung slightly
from the movement of the undressing.

The eight or ten girls at his end of the bar made way for him,
guiding him to a barstool merely by breaking ranks. The extremely large barman instructed him to have a drink, and he
couldn't have agreed more. He ordered a whisky.

'Four pounds, sir.' You didn't argue with that voice; if
anything you felt like saying, Is that all, can't you make it a bit
more, here, have seven pounds. It was an extremely small
whisky. He was now almost half-way through his roll.

'I'm sorry, I don't think I can afford to stand you all a round,'
he said apologetically to the girls around him. He had never
seen so many different-sized and different-breasted girls at the
same time in his life. It made him feel funny. It didn't make
him feel particularly dirty; it made him feel a bit as if he were in
a zoo.

'That's all right,' said the girl on his right. 'Ours are on the
house.' They were mostly drinking orange juice. He took a sip
of his whisky. He felt the conversation was beginning to die.

'So, what do you all do?' he said nervously, as if he were at a
party. It was probably the least necessary question he asked in
his whole life. The girls giggled.

'And what do you do?' countered the one on his left, a dark
girl with a northern accent and breasts which seemed about
half-way between the two extremes on offer.

'I'm a . . . I'm a . . . ' One or two of them began to giggle
already. Presumably the men always lied, that was one of the

rules, and the girls always knew it. Finally he said, 'I'm a . . . couturier.'

They howled at that one, and a girl on the fringes of the fat man detached herself and moved across to Duffy's group. Conversation languished again. He was nearly at the end of the whisky.

'Right,' said the girl on his left. 'That's enough browsing. Which of us are you taking downstairs? The suspense is killing.'

'Oh.' Duffy reached for his whisky and gulped the final teaspoonful down. He felt shy about examining them all in front of one another, even if he had paid his twenty pounds. He ducked his head and said, 'Oh, well, you I suppose,' to the girl on his left.

They stood up, and as they did so the girl in the leotard pulled up her shoulder-straps and tucked her tits back into place. They'd stay there till the next customer. He followed the girl he'd chosen across the room towards the stairs. She was, he noted, wearing black velvet pants which finished at mid-calf level, so that he seemed to be following the legs of a gondolier; and below them, gold-strapped sandals with high heels.

As they walked downstairs, it seemed to get even darker. There was a strong smell of incense. They reached the other room pictured outside, the one with the separate booths and the slatted swing doors. After a little peering around, the girl found an empty booth and they settled in. She pressed a bell and said,

'What's your name, love?'

'Nick. What's yours?'

'Delia. Terrible name, innit? Call me something else if you want to. Most people do.'

'No, that's fine, it's . . . perfectly all right.' He didn't reckon he'd have much cause to use her name; there wouldn't be much shouting across crowded rooms during this encounter. A waiter appeared with two glasses and a quarter-bottle of champagne; it wasn't so much on ice as on melted water.

'Ten,' the girl whispered to him, and he counted out some more of Gleeson's money.

The girl poured two glasses and clinked with him. He drank from his; she put hers down on the table.

'Where j' get the clothes then?'

'D'you like them?'

'Yeah, I think they're really nice. They're really Fifties, aren't they?'

'Uh-huh.'

'Where j' get them?'

'Oh, this little shop I know. Does Fifties revival clothing.'

The girl smiled at him, almost a normal smile, he thought.

'Why the smell of mothballs, then?'

'That's just my cologne. That's coming back too. Haven't you heard of it – mothball cologne?'

'Yer kidding.'

'No. I'm not.'

'Yer funny.'

'Uh-huh.'

'You can hold me tits if you like.'

'Oh.'

'You paid for them, after all. That's why they're out. They're not for looking at.'

'Of course not.' It was, he supposed, marginally more exciting than being asked to hold a bag of caster sugar; she certainly knew how to drain the invitation of eroticism. He stretched out his hand and curled it round her right breast. She seemed almost relieved, as if the proprieties of the occasion were at last being observed.

He looked at the table. Apart from the champagne there were three things on it: a lighted candle; a bunch of exotic-looking flowers which he guessed were plastic; and a puffing joss-stick.

'They're real,' she said. She probably wasn't still talking about her tits.

'Are they?'

'Yeah – have a sniff.'

He would. He considered the logistics of it and realised he couldn't lean as far as the flowers without first removing his hand from Delia's breast; as it was he'd been sipping his champagne left-handed and getting in a tangle of arms every time. He released his grasp on her breast and bent his head towards the flowers. As he did so he caught a quick movement out of the corner of his left eye. He sniffed them; they smelled vaguely lush, though with the overlay of joss-stick it was hard to be precise.

He straightened up and returned his hand to her breast: again the right one, which was nearer; it seemed over-familiar, or complaining, to reach across for the far one.

'What sort are they?'

'Dunno. They're fresh. Fresh every day. Mr Dalby has them flown in every day. Flown in from abroad. Fresh flowers for my little flowers, he says.'

'Why did you throw your champagne away when I was smelling them?'

'Oh, to get rid of it and order another bottle. Actually, I don't really like the taste any more. I've gone right off it since I started working here. Would you like me to toss you off?'

'Er, not just now, I think.'

'It's ten if you're worried about the price. Look, quick, better order another bottle, here comes Mr Dalby.' She pressed the bell in the wall and Duffy took his hand off her breast to reach for his money. A man had come out of an office up a few stairs at the far end of the room, and was slowly walking along between the booths. He was being discreet, looking out of the corner of his eye, but his soft-footed presence made the girls leap to their bells and order more champagne.

'I'll drink yours as well this time, if you don't mind.'

'All right, but don't dawdle over it, you'll have to drink it as quick as if we was both drinking it.'

'All right.'

Mr Dalby was almost level with their booth. He walked a bit like an old man, but maybe that was because he was trying not to scare the customers. In fact he was about forty, with a round face and little round glasses and a pink complexion and a chalk-striped suit. Duffy looked away, and it wasn't punter's guilt that made him do so. Mr Dalby was the man in the drawer.

5

'Is that the boss?'

'Yeah, that's Mr Dalby.'

The second quarter-bottle of champagne arrived, leaving Duffy with six of Gleeson's pounds left.

'You been dahn the dogs?'

'What?'

'The dogs – that where you got all them pound notes?'

'No,' he said, 'Hardy Amies always pays me like this.' She giggled. He quite liked her. No, that was an exaggeration. He didn't mind her. He placed his hand, damp from the champagne bottle, back on her right breast. Were you allowed to rub, he suddenly thought, or was that extra? Not that he particularly wanted to.

'What's he like, Mr Dalby?'

'He's all right. He sticks by the rules. If you don't like the rules you don't have to work here, so that's fair enough.'

'Do you have to go to bed with him?'

'Yeah, course. Not very often. And he always pays you. You can say No if you like as well, that's one of the rules. Not that anyone would, of course.'

'Uh-huh.'

'And anyway he doesn't really like it much, so that makes it better for you.'

'He doesn't like it?'

'No, not really. He does it a lot, but he doesn't seem to like it.

He's the sort of fellow always puts two tonkies on first cause he's scared of catching something, know what I mean?'

'Mmm.'

'And then it's stick it in, pull it out, wipe it off and straight into a bath.'

'You're joking?'

'No. Straight up. He's got a little flat up there – office, bedroom, bathroom. He always runs the bath first, it's all part of his routine, so he can jump straight in afterwards.'

'What else does he do?' Did Mrs Boseley know all this, he wondered.

'Well, sometimes he sniffs some stuff before doing it.'

'What sort of stuff?'

'Well, there's two sorts. There's some stuff in a little capsule which he keeps by the bedside, and then just after he takes his socks off he sort of breaks it under his nose and sniffs it. And sometimes he gets some powder and sniffs that instead. But it doesn't seem to make him enjoy it any more.'

'And what do you do?'

'I just lie there waiting for him to get on with it. I mean, it's all preparations and then washing as far as he's concerned. Not that *I'm* complaining – I wouldn't mind if all my gentlemen were like that.'

Duffy was feeling very pleased with himself. He was beginning to feel glimmerings of understanding. After nights in Carol's cramped Mini, this was his reward. He felt good. Now, if he put some of his own money with the rest of Gleeson's . . .

'How much did you say you charged?'

Delia smiled at him in a puzzled way.

'Ten, love,' and her hand landed on his thigh in a commercial caress. Six of Gleeson's oncers, a fiver of his own, take back one of Gleeson's . . . he put it on the table. When she saw the blue five pound note she chuckled.

'Hey, Mister Big Spender.' Weren't men odd? You never could tell what they'd get off on. Here he was, all friendly enough to talk to but not exactly the grope of the month, and then tell him about fucking Mr Dalby and all of a sudden he's finding he's got deeper pockets than he knew.

Apart from anything else, Duffy was glad to get the waist-band of his trousers undone; it had been killing him. He unzipped his fly and let her dig out his cock for him. Quickly and diligently, she milked him out on to the carpet.

Duffy thought, no wonder they need so many joss-sticks, what with the stuff that gets dumped on this carpet; first the champagne, then the spunk. Maybe they have carpet tiles down there, where it was too dark to see, and change them once a week. The candle was burning down. The unnamable flowers looked just as fresh, though he still couldn't smell them. Duffy wondered, just wondered, who freighted the joss-sticks.

The exhilaration of the previous evening had already ebbed away by the time Duffy got Hendrick's call.

'Been wondering how you've been getting along.'

'Oh, fine, Mr Hendrick, fine. Bit of this and that, lots of surveillance.' (They liked that word, even if most of them couldn't pronounce it.) 'Lots of sitting around in cars, you know what the job's like.'

'Yes. But have you been getting anywhere?'

'Well, I'm a lot more clued up than when I started.'

'It's quite expensive, hiring you, Mr Duffy.'

'Uh-huh.'

'And you haven't caught my thief.'

'No.'

'And there haven't been any more thefts since you arrived.'

'Now, Mr Hendrick, you wouldn't want there to be, would you?'

'No, of course not.'

'So maybe my presence there is putting them off.' Duffy felt this was a wonky line as he produced it.

'Yes, but if you're putting them off, then they aren't stealing anything and you aren't catching them, are you?'

'No.' Hendrick was clearly all logicked up at this time of the morning. It wasn't fair. Duffy was still on his first cup of coffee.

'You see, I can't afford to pay you just to be there to see that they *don't* steal things.'

'Of course not.'

'I mean, that would be even more expensive than just letting them help themselves once a month to whatever they fancied.'

Duffy grunted.

'And you have been there almost a month, haven't you?'

'Well, it must be coming up for their time again, then.'

'I don't know whether to hope it does or hope it doesn't.' Ah, Hendrick's logic was beginning to tire at last.

'Put it this way, Mr Hendrick, it is entirely your decision, and naturally I respect whatever you think it's best to do. I would just ask for a little more time, though. I can see your point of view – you haven't had anything for your money yet. On the other hand, you haven't lost anything for your money yet. And I take it my work in the shed is satisfactory.'

'Oh yes, quite satisfactory. In fact, Mr Duffy, if you were thinking of giving up your present employment . . . '

'That's very kind of you. So' (you always had to get the next line in before the client did) 'we'll leave it as it is for a bit, shall we?'

'I suppose we'd better.'

As he rang off, Duffy thought, well, that's a bit more time; but not much. And if the worst comes to the worst I could always tell him I've got a criminal record; that way he'd probably promote me straight over Mrs Boseley's head.

It was funny, he reflected, as he drove to work. Some bits of it always were funny, that was what kept you going. The eager guy from the Gemini had ended up painting his insides into the Watches box; and the girl in Dude's had been the one who'd drawn the double cream. You'd never have guessed *that*, said Duffy firmly to himself; you'd never have guessed *that* if I'd given you the options beforehand.

But in other ways, it wasn't particularly funny, or neat, or comprehensible. As he drove to work, the jumbos were following him again. Duffy read the news to himself. 'All 352 people . . . ' 'All 113 people . . . ' 'All 2,345,918 people . . . ' That was always how they began the news of aircrashes. Never just '254 people . . . ' And as soon as Duffy heard that first *All* on the radio, he knew how the sentence was going to continue: ' . . . were killed when a DC-10 of Cockroach Airways flew straight into the side of a mountain near Lake Honky Tonky. Wreckage was strewn over a wide area. As far as is known the plane was on course and experienced no mechanical trouble . . . ' Presumably they just had a tape ready and fed in the minor details that made this crash different from any other. And always they began with that *All*.

As the Cockroach Airways jumbos queued up for their go at crashing, Duffy thought about yesterday's exhilaration and today's disappointment. The exhilaration came from being carried away by a hypothesis; the disappointment from examining the facts as he knew them to be. And they were still uselessly thin.

Start at the beginning. Hendrick had some goods stolen; that we believe, don't we? Yes, for want of any contrary evidence. McKay was crashed. *No* – McKay crashed, that's all you know: he sideswiped something, or something sideswiped him, and he ran off the road and is all fucked up in hospital. Could have been accidental, could have been deliberate; just because the other vehicle didn't stop doesn't make it a contract job; people often don't stop if they think they can get away with it.

Next, he got fifty quid in his locker and six calculators. To bribe him into something, to pay him off for something, to set him up for something? He couldn't tell, and his exchange with Gleeson under the bonnet of the van had probably closed off finding out any more about that.

Next, there were two people working for Hendrick with criminal records. So – the sun still rises in the east.

Next, nothing more had been stolen since he got there. That

could mean that he'd been fingered; or that McKay had been the thief; or that there hadn't been anything particularly tempting since he'd arrived.

Next, he'd had a good look round the shed on his own, had gone through the accounts, kicked a few packing cases, snuffled about, and come up with nothing. He'd also sat outside a few houses and come up with nothing there too. Except . . .

Except that beyond this point it was all hypothesis, probably based on the fact that he disliked Mrs Boseley as unreservedly as she did him. And some prejudice like that always got the old hypotheses scurrying off in all directions.

Mrs Boseley kept a photograph of Mr Dalby in her office drawer; face down. Mrs Boseley went up to Dude's with her hair loose, and stayed there an hour. Mr Dalby – he'd checked in his notebook – was one of Hendrick Freight's regular customers. Mr Dalby popped the odd capsule of amyl nitrate before getting on the job; perhaps he had ignition trouble. So what else was new? And what did a really smart fellow conclude from this set of facts? That Mrs Boseley was having an affair with Mr Dalby, which was quite understandable: if you lived in Rayners Lane with an invalid husband and had once had a fruity career as a stewardess, wouldn't you occasionally fancy putting your hair down and taking a trip into town? It would be worth driving all that way for *that*, wouldn't it? It always seemed to be. Duffy had driven further himself. And this would explain why the photo was face down – the touch of shame, the decorum of adultery. And as for only staying an hour, well, the girl had given Duffy the lowdown on Mr Dalby's brevity of indulgence. Besides, he had a business to run, especially at the time Mrs Boseley had called: must get out there and keep the girls hitting those bells. Duffy felt almost sorry for Mrs Boseley.

Argued this way, the hypothesis – and Duffy's assumption that there were two strands of action at Hendrick Freight, not one – fell apart. The only thing that made him want to keep on nagging at it was his dislike for Mrs Boseley's character and Mr Dalby's prices. Fifty quid – no, fifty-four quid – for a hand-job, a small amount of champagne and a whisky which you could only see was there because it was coloured brown; ask for a vodka at the bar and they could give you an empty glass and you wouldn't be able to tell the difference.

So, what had seemed, in the exhilaration of drink and spending someone else's money and not having his clothes laughed at and feeling like getting lucky, to be some sort of a break, now struck Duffy as little more than an extra insight into the way shits lived. Nothing more than that. If he wanted to hold on to the job – and it did keep him off the streets – he would either have to find out more, or make something happen.

Or both, perhaps. At lunchtime he rang Willett and invited himself over after work for a question-and-answer session; still just background work, but maybe with a more precise focus than before. And in the afternoon he got down to some thinking about the morning's telephone conversation with his irritatingly logical employer. Hendrick said there hadn't been a theft since Duffy was hired, and his tone seemed almost complaining. Well, if a client wanted a theft, who was Duffy to stand in his way?

'Catch any stuffers this week?' asked Duffy as they sipped coffee in the bazaar of the imperial city. Willett gave a creased smile.

'No – couple I wouldn't have minded having a good rummage in, though.' He gave his old Waterguard's grin. 'Best thing that happened was to a mate of mine down at Gatwick. Bit of old Pakki-smuggling.'

'That still going on?'

'Sure – God knows why, but they still want to come. Costs them about five thousand each, too, that's the going rate. Some of them do it on H.P. – you know, something down at the start, and then a few quid a week over twenty years or so. Twenty years when the guy they're paying can decide to up his rate, or just turn them in if he gets bored. They must really want to come.'

'Well, it's a Tory paradise here, isn't it?'

'I'll ignore that one, Duffy. Some of them, of course, never get here. They get as far as Rotterdam, hand over all their money, and then the little boat in the night never turns up; the decent chap who promised to help them and told them how scandalous the immigration laws were has just buggered off. There's a lot of penniless Pakkis in Rotterdam.' He nodded sagely, as if advising Duffy not to go off and join them.

'Anyway, this mate of mine down in Gatwick. He has this great container of stuff to search. All jumbled up. You know, you can hire part of a container, you don't have to have the lot, and this one had been split up among lots of firms, and there were all sorts of cases and packages and whatnot in it, and it was pissing down with rain, and he really thought, you know, you get those nights sometimes – he thought What *am* I doing here? So he just bashes on this big cabinet and says, "You all right in there?" and a Pakki voice comes back, "Yes, fine, thank you very much".'

Duffy burst out laughing, then guiltily tried to calm down as a tiny Asian cleaning-woman floated past. It was pathetic, of course, and all that; but it was fucking funny as well.

'That's the way it is, you see,' went on Willett. 'The blokes we're dealing with are either too clever by half, or they're so thick you feel sorry for them. And even the ones who are normally clever often turn thick when they decide to smuggle something; they're just not up to it. Take all the Iranians we were picking up last year. Bloody smart back in their own country, doing well, nice pot of money, then along comes the old Ayatollah Whatsit. Bad news, time to leave. Only trouble is, currency restrictions: you can leave, the old man says, but two Crunchy bars each, that's the limit. So they think, aha, well, we won't take it out in money, let's take it out in heroin, after all the Ayatollah doesn't think much to that anyway, so he isn't going to mind us taking some with us.

'They fill up a suitcase, bung in the heroin, jump on a plane, and turn up here. And what do we see? One wealthy Iranian businessman in a lightweight suit, straight off a flight from Teheran, just a small case and sweating like a pig. He's only just realised that if we catch him and pop him back on the next plane, it's not going to be Oh, you are a naughty boy, it's going to be a couple of quick paragraphs from the Koran, and then Bang bang. So the fellows with gold rings round their sleeves take a quick dekko at him, then look at each other and say, "After you, Claud; no, after you, Cecil".'

Duffy nodded, and got down to business.

'If I was you . . . No, if I was *me* and looking for something, where would I look?'

'That's a bit vague.'

'If I thought something was coming in, but didn't know what it was.'

'That's still too vague, Duffy. I mean, you'd have to use your nose, wouldn't you? And you can only learn nose, so that wouldn't be much good. Still, if you want to know, you start by standing there and seeing how people react to you as they go past.'

'It's hard to do that with freight.'

'Ah, now he mentions it. Well, freight's always a bugger. There's the very occasional tip-off, and the usual amount of luck, which means not very much. And grey matter still works. Sometimes you spot something suspicious when you go round a shed.'

'For instance?'

'Well, say there's something wrapped up in hessian, you might give it a gentle kick, put the toe-cap in, and see how it feels underneath. Normally you'd expect cardboard. So if you feel metal underneath, you start wondering: why wrap something in hessian when it's already in a tin box? So you might very well want to take a gander.

'Or you might get a line on things from the documentation. Why is someone importing four thousand cuddly toys from

Ghana when you happen to know there isn't a cuddly-toy industry in Ghana? You're looking for things that don't feel right. Why is someone bothering to import something when the shipping costs exceed the declared value of the goods? That sort of thing.'

'Lots of paperwork.'

'Well, we do have LACES. The computer.'

'But a computer can't tell you what to search.'

'You'd be surprised. I mean, often that's exactly what it does do. It sorts the stuff into channels for us – like the green and red channels for passengers. With freight it's Channel One, scrutiny of documents; Channel Two, scrutiny of documents and examination of cargo; Channel Three, clearance within one hour.'

'How does it decide?'

'Well, every airline gives us a cargo manifest for every flight, saying what they're carrying, and we feed it into LACES. We have a read-through of it at the same time – the cargo's usually still in the air at the time, sometimes it hasn't even left – and if we spot something we think we ought to take a look at, we key in a 97. That's an inhibitor: tells the computer to route the cargo to Channel Two, which is then done automatically.

'But it does a lot by itself as well. There's a whole lot of things keyed in all the time: suspect importers, for instance, or cargo from what we call the Badlands. All new importers are picked out automatically the first couple of times, and so are any one-offs that come through. Plus what I just told you about: if the declared value of the goods being shipped is less than the shipping costs, the computer turns that up for us, and we take a look. Often that means quite innocuous things get examined, like samples of booze being sent from a factory abroad back to the home country for analysis. Still, it's a useful check.'

'What about random sampling?'

'Oh, the computer does that for us too. It diverts something

93

like one per cent through Channel Two on a purely random basis. We get a printout, an E1, telling us the reason the stuff's been picked out. Then we take a look.'

'Hm.' This might have made things easier for the likes of Willett, but it didn't seem to help Duffy much. 'So nobody smart would use a one-off shipment for smuggling? They'd know you'd look more closely at it.'

'They might, yes, if they knew how we worked. But then . . .'

'. . . ?'

'Well, it's all bluff and double-bluff, isn't it? I mean, sure we look at the one-offs as a matter of routine. But we also have to look at the regular stuff just because it's regular. You have to be always on the hop. It's like them being either very clever or very thick. Or like the way they hide stuff. To start with, they put things in the least obvious place, then for a bit in the most obvious place, then back in the least obvious place.'

'What would you look for if you were me?'

'Well, I don't know. You're still vague as vague. But if you know what you're looking for, then you can work a bit from the origin of the goods and their destination. And it's always a good idea to look out for something that's being freighted unnecessarily. I mean, it's expensive, air freight: so you should think, Why are they importing this fruit from Ghana when they can get it more cheaply from Italy, or wherever, so you have a bit of a rummage and maybe you find something. It's like that big drugs haul they had down at London docks. There were a couple of Volkswagens coming in on a boat from Malaysia; perfectly normal, all the papers were O.K., no problems. Except one of the officers thought: Why are they importing these two rather old Beetles when the shipping costs are greater than the cost of buying similar cars over here? So they stripped them down and found them full of Chinese Number Three.'

Duffy felt the conversation was drifting in one particular direction; that was the one he'd intended, but he thought he'd better clear some ground first. He went and got them a couple more coffees.

'Let me start at another angle. What do they kill for? What do they think about killing for?'

'Oh – varies. Depends how nasty they are. Depends what you've done to them. Depends how easy it is to do it. I don't come across it myself, but then I wouldn't.'

'Gold?'

'Nnnn. Not much of that about nowadays. Most of the money stuff is all paperwork. You know, altering documents so that the goods appear to have come from one place instead of another; then you pay less import duty or whatever. That sort of thing. Gold's really tight nowadays. Not like the Fifties – that was the Gold Rush. You'd have pilots and stewardesses with special shirts, everyone was mad and greedy; just one run, they'd say, and I can retire. Just one run. And sometimes they'd try and take a double load, and just keel over with nerves. Or heat. One chap I remember, keeled over on the tarmac at Calcutta Airport. Shirt pockets full of gold. Got seven years in Calcutta jail. Lasted a couple, then just died. Poor bugger.'

'Porn?'

'No. It's not that nasty a business, from what I hear. Not that I see too much – the big shipments come in by road. It's so heavy. We don't get much here except private consumption stuff: half a dozen fladge mags down the Y-fronts, that sort of thing.'

'So, if – and it's only if as far as I know – someone, say, arranged an accident for someone, then, unless it was personal, it might be what . . . drugs?' After the meandering of the sentence Duffy pronounced the last word sharply.

'There's more *ifs* in that sentence than when I'm trying to get the wife into bed, Duffy.'

'Well, let's assume some ifs.'

'O.K., what do you want to know?'

'Where would I look?'

'Turn it round. You're not you, you're them. Where would *you* put it?'

'Dunno, that's why I asked you.'

'Well, think about it.' Willett suddenly seemed severe, as if Duffy were one of his stumbling assistant officers who'd just let the French Connection through. 'You tell me how you'd bring it through, and I'll tell you an improvement on what you suggest.' He was proposing a game, Duffy realised. He sipped his coffee and imagined himself – with extreme difficulty – on a plane descending to Heathrow. *All* 256 *passengers . . .* was what came into his head.

'I'd . . . I'd have a special pocket sewn in my clothes.'

'Go to Pakistan,' said Willett dismissively. 'They'll sell you ready-made shoes, all built up with special compartments in the heels and soles. Buy them with or without the dope inside. Of course, we'd pick you up straight away. Had one only the other day: Pakki and his small son, teetering along, both wearing them. Walking awkwardly, but never looking at their feet. No problem.'

'I'd dress smart and walk through the customs next to a hippie.'

'Not bad – if you can find one on your flight. They're not as common as they used to be. I'll tell you a better one. You hire a couple of couriers, one smart, one a bit scruffy; actually, it doesn't matter what they look like, but you need two. You give a small amount of stuff to one, and all the rest to the other. Then you tip off the customs about the first guy. They wouldn't think there'd be *two* couriers on the same flight.'

Duffy was impressed. Willett meant him to be.

'I'd bring it in by car.'

'What, in the boot? Don't make me laugh. Not when compressed cannabis resin can be shaped like fibreglass. You can get yourself a whole new car wing. Like in *Goldfinger* – only much more plausible.'

'I'd . . . fly in from some unsuspicious airport.'

'There aren't any. All airports are suspicious. You might

have two passports, though – one to get you to Paris and back like a weekender and one to fly you on from there to pick up the stuff. That's quite clever.'

'I'd check in two suitcases with identical sets of clothes, one with the stuff in. Then if I were stopped, I could go back to the carousel and pick up the other suitcase.' Duffy was quite pleased with this, but Willett only chuckled.

'Moses was busting them with that trick crossing the Red Sea. What about the baggage tickets? Anyway, you're only allowed one bag each on a lot of flights nowadays. What's more, if you did, you wouldn't put the same clothes in each case. The case you left on the carousel would have *your* clothes in; the one you took through should be full of dirty knickers and Tampax spilling out when we opened it, so that it *obviously* wasn't yours. How about that?'

There was a competitive light in Willett's eye. Duffy felt the rules of the game were a bit unfair. After all, he'd never even been in a plane, and wasn't going to start now. He said rather grumpily,

'I give up.'

'They don't.'

No doubt Willett was trying to teach him something. No doubt he was right to try to do so. Duffy gave his friend the benefit.

'So where do I look?'

'I wish there was an easy answer. You look everywhere. There's nowhere it can't be – within reason. If it's cannabis, then it's bulky, you've got that on your side. But if it's hard stuff . . . You can get half a million quid's worth of heroin between the back light of a car and the boot. That's where you'd have to be looking, and that's what it's worth to them to hide it.'

'The hardest places.'

'And the easiest places. And the hard–easy places. What do opium sticks make you think of? Cigarettes, right. So you wouldn't look for them there. We had opium sticks the other month hidden inside the cigarettes in a sealed carton of duty-free Marlboro, which as far as anybody could see had been bought in transit at Frankfurt.'

'Has anything changed much since I was last chasing the stuff? Like where it comes from. Is the Golden Triangle still producing as hard as ever?'

'It's a quadrangle, Duffy. Bits of Red China as well. No, the stuff's just the same – only there's more of it. Iran's pretty well closed down – I suppose you have to hand that to the old Ayawhatsit. But as against that, the Pakkis have just cracked how to refine theirs much better. Their stuff used to be crummy, I expect you remember; the best was only about thirty per cent. Now they've made the breakthrough: it's up to ninety, all of a sudden. Swings and roundabouts, isn't it – except that they're making the roundabouts go faster.'

Duffy felt glum. Five, six, seven years ago he'd pounded up and down Gerrard Street, in and out through the Chinese area of Soho like one keen young copper. He used to imagine wizened old Chinamen in back rooms puffing dreamily away at opium pipes, only disturbed by the zealous young Duffy bursting through the door, truncheon in hand, quipping, 'Not Rothman's Number Two again, sir?' It had all seemed picturesque; at first, anyway. He used to stroll along Gerrard thinking: Down these chow mein streets a man must go. None of it had hit home until a couple of years later.

'Dead babies,' said Willett sharply. Duffy looked up, and saw no longer the familiar garrulous old joker, but a serious customs officer.

'Dead babies,' he repeated. 'I can imagine what you're thinking, Duffy, and I've had it a lot of times myself. I'll never find it, you think. What's the point – if they want it that badly, let them have it. I catch myself going down that track sometimes, and I always stop myself before I get too far by thinking about dead babies.' He took a swig of coffee. 'You'll remember there's quite a lot of heroin goes across the border between Thailand and Malaysia? Well, couple of years ago the smugglers came up with a new system. They buy babies. Sometimes they kidnap them, but often they just buy them: they say there's some rich, childless woman in Singapore wants to adopt a kid. Why shouldn't a poor peasant sell one of hers; she's got enough and some over. So the peasant sells one: seems a good opportunity, like sending the kids to college. But of course they don't ever get to this imaginary rich childless woman in Bangkok. The smugglers kill them, take out their internal organs, and stuff them with bags of heroin. Then they give them to a "mother" who cradles them in their sleep and carries them over the border. Simple as that.'

Duffy felt sick, but Willett hadn't finished. 'Of course, it's got to look as natural as possible. So they only use babies which are under two years old – otherwise their sleeping pattern might seem unusual. And the other thing is – don't forget this, I don't – they always have to be got across the border within twelve hours of being killed. Otherwise the colour will have drained out of their faces and they won't be any use.'

Duffy didn't need the details – he didn't need them at all; but he knew it was good for him to have them, however sick they made him feel. Willett certainly knew how to get to him. So all he said was,

'Thanks.'

The only thing that stopped Duffy brooding at work the next day was planning his switch. From among the clients who regularly came to collect their own goods he picked out his target: a couple of pile-it-high, sell-it-cheap hifi villains. They were full of shoulder-slapping, bracelet-chinking, fell-off-the-back-of-a-lorry bonhomie, and wouldn't think twice about anything that came their way by mistake; in Duffy's opinion, they thought honesty was just a plant that grew in the garden.

Their pile of hifi equipment came in to a regular bay in the shed, quite near Duffy's corner; so far he'd always been the one instructed to load their van. In the course of the day, while seemingly doing no more than he was told to, Duffy managed to shift a small case of Japanese cigarette lighters across the shed until it was in the bay next to the hifi equipment.

The whole of Hendrick Freight always heard them coming: they drove with the side doors of their transit van hooked back, and Capital Radio at full blast. Their arrival was the nearest thing to an event in the week of loading and unloading. If the flashier of the two was driving, he'd always look for little patches of oil on the floor of the shed, and try to put the van into a skid by stamping on the brakes.

Towards the end of the afternoon they arrived with a roar and a squeal, backed the van up to their bay, turned the engine off but left the radio on. With a 'Hiya, wack' at Duffy they clattered off to flirt as successfully as anyone could with Mrs Boseley, and in the process exchange receipts with her. Duffy loaded up six boxes of tape-decks, six boxes of turntables, six boxes of tuners, six boxes of amplifiers, and one smaller case of Japanese cigarette lighters, from which he quickly ripped off the documentation: didn't want to give them an attack of conscience, however unlikely. He stuck the lighters between the turntables and the side of the van, so that they would be invisible when Gleeson checked off his list.

The hifi villains clattered out of Mrs Boseley's office, Gleeson wandered over with a clipboard and checked the van, the driver shouted, 'Didn't forget the smoked salmon, did you, wack?' at Duffy, who bellowed, 'It's under the seat', in reply, and they roared off. What they would make of the place where the lighters were stuffed Duffy didn't know; in all likelihood they didn't unload themselves; there was probably an old man with two withered arms employed to do that for them.

The lighters were due to be picked up the next day, and they were in Casey's area of the shed; so Duffy didn't need to worry about that. It could take care of itself.

With the switch safely concluded, and not much work for the rest of the day, Duffy started brooding again. He found himself gazing across at Mrs Boseley's blonde hair in the glass office and thinking violent, unprofessional thoughts for which there was at present no possible justification. All because Mr Dalby occasionally snorted a little coke before screwing his hostesses, and because Willett had told him various unpleasant truths.

Duffy's moral outlook had always been pragmatic. Three years in the force had made it more so, and it wasn't going to change now. He wasn't idealistic about the law, or about how it was implemented. He didn't mind a bit of give-and-take, a bit of blind-eye, a bit of you-naughty-boy-on-yer-bike and forget it. He didn't think the ends justified the means – except that sometimes, just occasionally, they did. He didn't believe all crimes were equal; some he couldn't get worked up about. But always, at the back, there were absolutes. Murder was one, of course, everyone agreed on that. Bent coppers was one; but then, Duffy had a little private experience of that, and could be expected to feel strongly. Rape was one; Duffy was disgusted how some coppers thought it was little more than a mild duffing up with a bit of pleasure thrown in. And heroin was one as well.

Seven years ago, Duffy had thought about sweet old Chinamen puffing away in poppy dreams; but he didn't think of that now. And Willett hadn't needed to push him with the dead babies, because Duffy was more or less there already, ever since Lesley. He'd laughed at the idea of Pakkis tripping over their built-up shoes, but it didn't mean he wouldn't cut their legs off at the ankles given half the chance. He knew all those colourful Chinese phrases they used about smoking heroin – chasing the dragon, playing the mouth organ, shooting the anti-aircraft gun – but they didn't charm Duffy; not since Lesley.

She had been a pretty, long-faced, serious-looking girl with dark hair and large eyes who had lived in the same block of flats as he had shortly after he'd been kicked out of the force. He vaguely fancied her but didn't do anything about it because he was all crazy from the shock of breaking up with Carol and the best he could do at the time was trail madly back to the Caramel

Club and drink too much and pick up any old rubbish and do whatever they wanted. She vaguely fancied him but didn't do anything about it because she was a junkie.

He remembered how avuncular, how responsible it had made him feel when she told him. He had a romantic picture of the two of them, bruised by the world, mending each other's hurts. Then she stole his camera. She came back and told him how sorry she was, it was just a question of priorities, and weighing her need against his camera there was really no argument. He accepted it immediately, it wasn't even a matter where he had to 'forgive' her or anything; he simply hadn't realised that junkies had weak characters. Now he knew; now he'd be prepared.

For an addict she was comparatively in control of her life. That's to say, she started thinking about what she needed to do to support her habit at least a day before her supplies ran out. Sometimes she stole; sometimes she worked in a massage parlour; sometimes she managed to get modelling jobs. Duffy continued to like her just as much as when they'd first met. Then she stole his tape recorder; and this time she was quite a bit less sorry. Why had he left it lying around his flat like that? He knew she only had to nick his duplicate key to get at it.

Sometimes she went off for cures which her family arranged, but always she came back. Her legs got thinner and her eyes got bigger; even the freckles on her face seemed to get bigger, stretching themselves into blotches. Her flat got filthier and her carpet began to stink. The carpet stank because when she pulled the syringe out of her arm with its residue of blood, she'd clean it by filling it up with water and then squirting it with a giggle at the patterns in the weave.

Duffy moved away because he knew that the cure rate for heroin addicts was one in ten, and that Lesley was going to be one of the nine. He moved away because he feared doing everything he could to help and still failing. It wasn't a decision he was proud of, but the self-obsession and weakness of addicts is catching: how can I defend *my*self, you begin to think after a while. He moved away because he was fond of her and didn't ever want to hear that she had died. She was twenty-two.

At one end of the chain there were dead babies in Thailand; at the other end there were Lesleys fixing themselves to death. She'd told him once that her one great fear wasn't dying, but that soon she'd have nowhere left to fix. The veins in her arms had gone; the veins in her legs had gone; she was fixing in her wrists and hands at the moment, which was more painful than she'd imagined possible. Soon, she said, she'd be fixing in her groin.

Duffy thought he'd hang around Hendrick Freight for a bit longer; just in case.

6

The next afternoon there was a sudden bustle at work. Duffy was looking down the shed from his dunce's corner when Mrs Boseley came skidaddling out of her office, pushing the door open with her right hand and still clutching the telephone in her left.

'Gleeson,' she yelled, 'GLEESON.'

She went back into her office and shut the door. Duffy could see her phone conversation taking a rather animated course for the next couple of minutes. Then she put the phone down, Gleeson arrived, and they closeted themselves together for a good ten minutes. After that Mrs Boseley picked up the phone again and made a call. Gleeson came out of the office and strode over to Casey's area of the shed. Duffy concluded that things were looking up. He ambled over himself. As he arrived, Casey was ripping open the top two press-buttons of his shirt. He pointed to the CUT HERE and made a slicing motion with the edge of his hand.

'Guides' honour,' he said, and did a wolf-cub salute to Gleeson.

'Fucking look some more,' said Gleeson.

Duffy coughed.

'Excuse me, Mr Gleeson. Anything the matter?'

'Fuck off, Duffy.'

'Anything I can do to help?'

'Fuck off, Duffy.'

He turned and began to wander off.

'No, just a minute. Help Casey search. Two half-brains are better than one, I suppose.'

'Charming,' muttered Duffy as Gleeson marched off to consult Mrs Boseley again.

'What are we looking for?'

'Case of sparks.'

'Ah. Get lost, did it?'

Casey didn't answer except by kicking a tea chest. Duffy assumed that meant Yes. Kick the tea chest for Yes; punch the packing-case for No; butt your head against the refrigerated container for Don't Know. That was probably the local vocabulary.

'Who were they for?'

'Mucks.' This was presumably Casey's abbreviation for Muxton and Walker.

'Who loaded them?'

Casey grunted indeterminately, but Duffy already knew the answer.

'Who signed them out?'

'Gleeson.'

'Who drove them?'

'Gleeson.'

Better and better, Duffy thought. He hadn't counted on that bonus. Normally, if the customer didn't collect, one of Hendrick's two drivers delivered the goods. That day, one of them had been off sick, the other had a heavier schedule as a result, and that morning Gleeson had obviously decided to do the delivery to Muxton's himself.

Duffy was still pretending to help Casey look for the missing case of sparks when a bottle-green XJ6 drove into the shed and parked in the most inconvenient place. Hendrick got out, looking extremely pissed off. After ten minutes in the eyrie, he, Mrs Boseley and Gleeson all came over to the area where Duffy, Casey, and now Tan as well were pretending to search. They were only pretending now, because they'd combed the whole of Casey's area twice and it was perfectly obvious that the sparks had flown – upwards or wherever.

'Afternoon, Mr Hendrick,' said Duffy as the three of them arrived. He was, after all, meant to be his ex-odd-job-man. 'Sorry to hear about this spot of bother.'

'Fuck off, Duffy,' said Gleeson before his boss could open his mouth, 'just fuck off back to your corner.'

Duffy tried looking phlegmatic, as if this was the sort of way Gleeson always treated him (not that it wasn't), in the hope that Hendrick might give his shed foreman a little talking-to about industrial relations. It was a distant hope; but Duffy's line in such circumstances was, Anything to stir it a bit.

As he stood in his corner he thought what he'd give for a duplicate set of invoices for the goods freighted to Dude's. He'd taken a good scout round in the course of the day, and read lots of bits of documentation stuck to cases, and loitered for a while in the refrigerated section in case he could make out the flowers whose scent was destined to be drowned by joss-sticks; but all to no avail.

At 5.30 he was changing by his locker when Tan came up to him.

'Mrs Boseley want see you before you go,' he said.

Aha. A regal audience. He finished changing, and bounded up the steps to her office.

'Oh, take a seat, please, Duffy. I won't be a minute.'

She bent over some paperwork and appeared to be adding up a line of figures. She did it once; she did it twice; then she sighed, and fished out a calculator from her top drawer. Duffy noticed that it was the same brand as the six he had left behind the cistern in the Gents, but he didn't jump to any conclusions. Or rather, he jumped to them straight away, and then rejected them. Whatever Mrs Boseley was messing with, he guessed, it wouldn't be just a little something to help her do her sums.

He glanced round her office. It looked much like any man's office, except that there wasn't a girlie calendar. Why didn't they make dirty calendars with men on them? All they seemed to make, if Mrs Boseley was anything to go by, was National Trust calendars.

Hey, come on, I've been here ten minutes, I could be dodging the jumbos on the M4 by now. He looked out into the shed. The double doors were closed for the night. Everyone seemed to have gone home. Except for him and Mrs Boseley. What *did* the E stand for? Elizabeth? Elspeth? Eva? Yes, probably Eva – changed her name to that of her great heroine, Eva Braun. Dyed her hair to look as Aryan as possible. What did she want to see him for? he wondered. She couldn't . . . oh no, that would be silly, wouldn't it? That would be just too corny. Handsome lady office manager falls for muscular young manual worker. Her initial air of frostiness only a poor, sad mask to hide the feelings which lurked within her . . . Secretly, she longed to . . .

Come on, Duffy, that's enough of that. And if she did, you know what you'd be? Sodding embarrassed for a start. You wouldn't know where to put yourself. You've never exactly appealed to that type of lady, have you? Not exactly a regular feature of your track record, are they?

So it was a surprise when Mrs Boseley finally laid down her calculator, looked up, and smiled. She did look better when she smiled, there was no denying that. The only fly in the ointment was that she wasn't smiling at Duffy; she was smiling past his shoulder.

'All locked up,' said Gleeson. The phrase gave Duffy a jolt: it took him straight back to his early days in the force, when he found such lines gave him an extra bit of swagger. 'On yer bike,' he'd gruff at a clearly bikeless hobo curled round the remnants of a bottle of sweet sherry; 'Yer locked up,' he'd shout at some particularly nasty bit of fighting rough, and just pray he didn't get the reply, 'You and who else?'

Duffy hoped he didn't show any reaction to Gleeson; hoped he just carried on staring with dulcet expectation at Mrs Boseley, as if she were about to award him a wage rise. When he heard Gleeson turning the key, however, he thought he had the right of any other normal citizen to swivel in his chair and issue a long, puzzled glance. Gleeson pocketed the key and came and stood behind Duffy's chair. Duffy didn't like that. It reminded him of the sort of coppers who enjoyed doing that to people they were questioning; and it reminded him of what occasionally happened when they did.

'Any complaints, Mrs Boseley?' he enquired, like any other normal employee who's been kept late, locked in, and has a big man with mutton-chops standing right behind his chair. She didn't deign to reply. Don't give up, he said to himself, keep the dialogue going – that's what they said whenever there were those street sieges, wasn't it? 'We are keeping the dialogue going with the gunmen.' Duffy decided to keep the dialogue going. It didn't strike him who was taking which role.

'I hope there haven't been, Mrs Boseley. Any complaints, I mean. I'm really enjoying my work here, you know. I meant to pop by and say so only the other day, but I looked in your office, and you were . . . you were on the phone.'

Mrs Boseley finally seemed to be giving attention to his presence, though not, as far as he could tell, to his words. She looked as if she were going to speak. He waited dutifully. She couldn't be going to sack him, could she?

'You're a man of many talents, Mr Duffy.'

Oh, well he didn't expect her to say *that*. If only Gleeson weren't there he might think she *was* about to make a pass at him.

'Yes, M'm?' Why did he never know what to call her?

'Principal among which, in my view, is the ability to mow concrete.'

'. . .?'

'You mow concrete, Mr Duffy.' It was spoken in the tone of one reminding a recalcitrant child about a multiplication table. Nine sixes, you know you know nine sixes, Mr Duffy.

'Beg yours?'

'You mow concrete. Up and down. And all the concrete

clippings go into the concrete box on the front of the mower. Wuuuuaaah, Wuuuuuaaah,' went Mrs Boseley all of a sudden, imitating the noise of a lawn mower. 'Or maybe – maybe you use an electric: then of course you don't have a concrete box on the front do you? You just have a rotary thing, don't you, and all the little bits of concrete go flying out of the side, and you leave them lying on the top and that acts as a fertiliser. Is that what you use?'

Duffy was bewildered. She was cracking up. All that wielding of a watering can in Rayner's Lane had finally cracked her. He squirmed round in his seat and looked at Gleeson by way of enquiry, but he only seemed to be staring back at Mrs Boseley in a headily admiring fashion, as at some prophet who promised to teach him how *he* could part the waters, too, and no sweat. When Gleeson became aware of Duffy's movement he reached down a fat palm and twisted Duffy's head back to face Mrs Boseley.

'I think we're on different wavelengths, Mrs Boseley,' he stammered.

'No, I don't think so, Duffy. You mow concrete. At least I think you do. Let me put it to you directly: do you mow concrete, Mr Duffy?'

'NO,' he replied loudly. He'd had enough of this. She looked disappointed. At least, she acted looking disappointed, which wasn't at all the same thing.

'Oh dear, I'd quite counted on you mowing concrete. You see, you said you did at your interview.'

Duffy looked blank.

'I asked you what your qualifications were and you said you did odd jobs for Mr Hendrick. I asked you what. You said you . . . lifted things. I remember letting that pass, though I did want to ask whether your expertise extended to putting things down again as well, or whether we were being asked to hire someone who went around all the time with stuff stuck in his hands because he hadn't yet learnt about putting down. And then I asked you if you mowed Mr Hendrick's lawn.' Uh-huh, thought Duffy, or rather he thought UH-FUCK-A-DUCK-HUH loud inside his head. 'And you said you did.' Duffy remembered the inexplicable sense of unease that he'd had when he'd visited Hendrick and looked out through his kitchen window at the children playing on the slide. Standing up on the top of it. Maybe he'd thought he was feeling uneasy about the kids falling off, but he wasn't; he must have been feeling uneasy about the future of Duffy.

'Now Mr Hendrick's lawn, as you would know if you had ever been anywhere near Mr Hendrick's house, is not made of the usual grass. Part of it is made of crazy paving and part is made of concrete. I engaged you, Mr Duffy, on the firm understanding that you could mow concrete. I'm very disappointed in you.'

'I'll learn,' Duffy found himself saying, 'I'm sure I can learn.' There was a faint, nasal snigger from behind him, a stern glance from Mrs Boseley which went over his shoulder, and then a hard, flat-handed clout across the top of his head from Gleeson. It hurt. It wouldn't have hurt at all if he'd known it was coming. That, doubtless, was the point.

'I don't think you'll learn quickly enough for me; it's a very difficult trade to learn. I don't think you'll master it quickly enough. If I hire a concrete-mower, Mr Duffy, I expect to get a concrete-mower. I'm afraid I'm going to have to dispense with your services.'

'Oh dear,' said Duffy. Oh dear not about being sacked – was he being, anyway? – but about the rest of it.

'But before you go, just tell us all about yourself.' Mrs Boseley put on what was quite clearly meant to be a violently insincere smile. She was quite an actress, Duffy had to hand it to her. Maybe it came from years of traipsing up and down the aisle with a 'Would you like tea or coffee, sir?' always on your lips, and getting pissed off with the fat men in bursting jackets with snowdrifts of dandruff on their shoulders quipping, 'I'd rather have you, darling' as if they were the first man ever to say it; and if at first you gave a polite half-amused smile, you would, after a few years of it and its equivalents, learn a real putdown of a smile, wouldn't you, a horrible parody of a smile, a fuck-you-Jack smile? Mrs Boseley had learnt one, anyway.

Gleeson hit him across the back of the head again. It hurt just as much as the first time.

'I'm just an ordinary fella,' he said.

'Who are you, Duffy?'

'I'm me.' It sounded weedy, lost.

'What are you, what do you do?'

'I'm me, I work, I work for you.' He put more pathos into it this time; it seemed to come quite naturally.

'You've never been to Mr Hendrick's house, have you?'

'Yes.'

Gleeson flat-slapped him again.

'You do something else, don't you?'

'No.'

'How did you meet Hendrick?' The 'Mr' had gone.

'I worked for him. Odd jobs.'

'Why were you loitering near the flowers today?'

'What?'

'Why were you loitering near the flowers today?'

'I don't know what you're talking about.'

'Why didn't you take the calculators?'

'I beg your pardon?'

'WHY DIDN'T YOU TAKE THE FUCKING CALCULATORS?' Mrs Boseley screamed at him. 'WHY DIDN'T YOU TAKE THE FUCKING CALCULATORS?' He hated that; he hated women screaming at him. He thought, That'll make Gleeson hit me again. But it didn't. It made Gleeson do something else instead. Something that made Duffy wish he'd been cuffed around the head after all. Something that made him feel altogether more uneasy.

It was a little click in his left ear, accompanied by a little pull on the lobe. He turned his head very slightly, and felt something cold against his flesh there. Out of the corner of his eye he saw Gleeson, who had moved round slightly to the side of him. When the second cold touch came, he worked out with no difficulty that Gleeson was gripping the gold stud in his left ear with a pair of pliers.

'Up,' said Gleeson, tugging gently with the pliers. Duffy didn't dispute the instruction. When he was standing, he was moved back a pace or two and his chair kicked away from behind him. Mrs Boseley came round from behind her desk and began to go through his pockets. He thought, briefly, of making a sudden dramatic leap at the woman, but he didn't fancy the consequences. And in any case, she was welcome to his pockets. Duffy wasn't smart for nothing. The notebook with the names of regular customers was at home; so was the spare key to the shed. She was welcome to a dirty handkerchief, some change, a small comb, a wallet which contained an out-of-date credit card and which was singularly lacking in little bits of white pasteboard announcing 'DUFFY SECURITY', a biro and half a packet of Opal Fruits. She piled all these between them on the desk.

'Down,' said Gleeson, kicking the chair back into Duffy's knees. He sat, a position which even without the local difficulty around his left ear gave Gleeson a considerable advantage. 'I might have to change hands now and then,' Gleeson informed him, 'But we won't try anything silly, will we?'

'I won't if you won't,' said Duffy.

'Right,' said Mrs Boseley, surveying the pile of Duffy's possessions as if she'd just tipped out half a dozen used contraceptives and a dead vole. 'Now let's start again.' Duffy looked at her with genuine apprehension. Part of this sprang from not knowing how to play it. He couldn't give them nothing. He couldn't give them everything up to his hypothesis. He'd better give them a bit, but not too much. And of course, how much he gave them depended a bit on Gleeson's activities round his left ear. Duffy was smart, but he was no braver than anyone else.

What he decided was, play it along for a bit, then as soon as Gleeson does anything that hurts, babble out all you're going to give them and then stick by it. Sticking by it was obviously going to be the tricky thing. What the pain, if it came, would be like, Duffy had no way of estimating. In fact, as he knew, you could pinch someone's earlobe quite hard and it didn't hurt; it was one of those semi-dead areas of the human body. So having his stud gripped by Gleeson's pliers didn't actually hurt – indeed, even the cold metal had now warmed up against his skin.

Or rather, it didn't hurt in his body. It hurt a lot in his mind. So it was better than it could have been and a lot worse, both at the same time. If Gleeson had been hurting him in a normal way – punching him in the face, say – and promising that it would get gradually worse until Duffy did or said something, then he'd know where he was, would be able to guess what he could endure. This way, it was the anticipation of pain, not present pain, that made him fearful; and that was a lot worse.

'Name?'

'Duffy.'

'What are you?'

'I work for you.'

'Where'd you meet Hendrick?'

'At his house.'

'Why were you loitering by the flowers?'

'I wasn'toooooooOOOOOOOWWWWWWWWWWWW.'

And that was just a little twist, a sudden half-turn on the pliers by Gleeson. It didn't feel very life-enhancing to Duffy.

'I never liked this fancy-boy's ear-ring of yours,' said Gleeson. 'But I never thought it would come in handy. That was just a little twist, just a little wiggle really. I wonder what would happen if I pulled a bit.'

Duffy thought, Shit, I hadn't known it was going to be like that. And knowing isn't going to make the next round any easier. I think it may be time to crack. He could feel Gleeson taking a fresh grip on the pliers. Yes, it's probably time to do the decent and crack.

'Name?'

'Duffy.'

He felt a little pull on his ear. Just a little pull hurt a great deal now. He closed his eyes as if he were making a last effort to hold himself together.

'What are you?'

He didn't answer, inviting another pull on the pliers, but not the sort of vicious, mind-blanking tug he'd get for an obvious lie, or for cheek. He wanted no more than a sort of this-is-a-reminder tug, the sort that would give him a justification for cracking. He got precisely that. He decided to crack.

'I run a security firm. Well, there's only me,' he babbled on. 'I'm a one-man band, I'm the firm, there's just me.' For that he got a sharp twist on the pliers, not quite a you-sodding-copper twist, but almost.

'Where'd you meet Hendrick?'

'In a club.'

'Why were you loitering by the flowers?'

'I was looking at the air waybills.'

He was pointing down at the desk, avoiding Mrs Boseley's eye in the way that villains who cracked avoided the copper's eyes: they told their shame to themselves, that was the theory, and the copper was just overhearing it. That way they still retained a scintilla of self-respect. Duffy's theory was slightly different: he could lie better with his head down.

'Right, now let's amplify things. Where was this club?'

'It's called the Alligator. It's in Fulham. It's a gay club. I met him there.'

Time for some broken-man-spills-all details. 'It's a nice place, very quiet, I was having a drink, he came in, we had a chat, he told me he was having thefts at work, I offered to help, he gave me the job. Then we decided to say I was his odd-job man, but I guess we didn't prepare our story well enough. I didn't think you'd interview me properly.'

'Odd-job man,' said Gleeson. 'I bet you were his odd-job man. Poof.' He switched the pliers to his left hand and belted Duffy again with his right. The blow jarred Duffy's head against the pliers; he thought he felt a trickle of blood easing its way down the side of his neck.

'Hey, lay off, will you. I'm answering. Lay off.' It was an appeal to Mrs Boseley, and it seemed to work.

'Yes, don't do that, Gleeson. There wasn't really any call for that.' She turned back to Duffy. 'And what did Hendrick say?'

'He said he'd been getting thefts. Fairly regular. About once a month. Said he didn't want to go to the police because they'd upset the shed.' A sudden thought came to Duffy: maybe Mrs Boseley had persuaded him not to go to the police? At first, anyway. And then maybe, after a while, he decided he'd go half-way.

'And what have you found out?'

'Well, it's got me rather baffled.' He didn't want them to think he was a particularly smart security man; and they were into a tricky area. 'I mean, I looked around a bit, and it seems to be a very efficiently run firm.'

'Spare us that,' said Mrs Boseley. Shit, overdoing the praise.

'Well, I mean *I* couldn't see how anyone could fiddle the system.' That put the blame back on his own slowness of mind, which was probably better by them. 'So I reckoned it was McKay. I reckoned he'd been using some system I couldn't work out because I wasn't around then. And that's as far as I'd got, except that now I suppose it must be Casey after all.' Though his head was still pointing at the little pile of his possessions on Mrs Boseley's blotter, he caught a glance on its way to Gleeson. *They'd* obviously thought it had been McKay as well; his switch yesterday had clearly thrown them.

'I don't think Casey's as thick as he looks. Did you know he'd got two O-levels? He told me over dinner. And the lighters went from his part of the shed. I don't know where the earlier stuff went from. But I reckon it's Casey. I was going to follow him home from work tonight, only I seem to have got held up.'

'Why were you loitering by the flowers?'

'I didn't know I was. I mean, no more than loitering by anywhere else. I was mooching around, working out the system, you know.' He very much didn't like the idea of telling them he thought there might be two fiddles, not one. But he had hopes. He had hopes he'd just about covered the exits. They were definitely worried by the latest theft, he could tell that. It had made them jumpy. He just had to keep them quiet, play them along a bit, and maybe he'd get out of the wood. That's what he thought.

'You're sacked, by the way.'

'What?'

'You're sacked. As of now.'

Duffy, rather to his surprise, said, 'Employment Protection Act.' He heard Gleeson give a nasal snigger of disbelief. 'Week's notice, I get a week's notice, I've got the right.'

'I don't think you've got any rights,' said Mrs Boseley. 'False pretences,' she added, as if quoting a subsection of the act.

'Week's notice,' repeated Duffy, as if quoting a different subsection. He didn't have the slightest idea what was in the act; and he guessed she didn't either. 'It's only fair. Week's notice. Then I might be able to stick it on Casey. And it wouldn't surprise the others so much. I think another week here and I could really stick it on Casey.' This was his best line. Presumably they knew, or at least thought, that McKay had been the thief; they'd had him crashed to stop him drawing attention to Hendrick Freight; and now they were jumpy that it might not have been McKay after all. Crashing two out of a firm of eight would be a bit much, even by their standards. But letting Duffy land Casey might appeal to them. 'You can sack me first thing tomorrow,' he said. 'I'll be late. Give me a week's notice in front of everyone.'

Mrs Boseley was thinking it over. Duffy thought he was almost home and dry.

'And you met Hendrick in a gay club?'

'Yes.'

'Are you . . . gay, as you call it?'

'Yes . . . sometimes.'

'And is Hendrick gay, as you put it?'

'Yes . . . sometimes.'

'Whatjer mean, *sometimes*?' said Gleeson ferociously from

behind him. 'You're a fucking poof or you aren't a fucking poof. You can't be both.'

Duffy should have said, Yes, sorry, Gleeson, you know about these things much better than me, I made a mistake, I am a fucking poof, that's the long and the short of it, I've always been a fucking poof, I am a fucking poof, a whole poof, and nothing but a poof. Instead, thinking he was home and dry, and so not thinking, he said,

'It's been scientifically proved that all men are to some degree bisexual.'

Half his head came off. First his ear came away completely, then half his jawbone, and a litter of teeth, and one eye and most of his nose and a good part of his brain. That was what it felt like. In fact, Gleeson had merely tugged on the pliers with the long clean pull of a gardener starting a motor mower. Duffy put his left hand up to his ear, beyond screaming, and felt the blood drip into his palm. And while his head was very slowly shuffling back into position, he felt the pliers clamp on his right earlobe, the naked one, the only one he had left. Oh my Christ, he thought. Gleeson bent to that ear and whispered,

'Not me, poof. Not fucking me.'

Duffy slowly looked up at Mrs Boseley. She didn't look in the least surprised. She didn't look pleased or displeased. She stared at him as if he were a newscaster on the television. He reached out his left hand, palm upwards, showing the blood; but all she did was pick his handkerchief off the blotter and hand it over to him. He swaddled it over his left ear and feared for his other one. Gleeson was holding it in a firmer grip than was absolutely necessary; but then he would, wouldn't he?

Fortunately, Mrs Boseley had made up her mind.

'You'll be late for work tomorrow, you'll be given a week's notice, you'll clear up Casey within that week, and you'll stay out of our way. That's enough, Gleeson, really; I wish you didn't enjoy it so much.'

The grip on his ear relaxed, then disappeared. Duffy wanted to say either, Thank you very much indeed, or, I'll fucking fix you, but wisely stuck to a middle course and stayed silent. He stood up, gathered his things from the blotter and stuffed them into his blouson. He heard the office door being unlocked behind him, but he didn't look at it, or at either of them. He clasped his handkerchief to his ear, ducked through the door, crossed the shed, pulled open the side door and went out into the evening. He thought that it would be night, that this was the only thing it would decently know how to be, after what he had been through. But it wasn't. It was still, cheekily, a bright, clear evening, and another fucking jumbo was coming in to land.

The houseman who stitched his ear at Uxbridge Hospital smelled faintly of lavender water.

'Well, it's not the best place to stitch, but then again it's not the worst. I don't need to tell you what the worst is.'

Duffy just wanted him to get on with it. He'd waited an hour and a half in casualty already, piqued that his injury was judged so unimportant, and that any old housewife who rolled up with half a television set embedded in her stomach could immediately jump the queue.

'ow,' he said, loudly. He'd run out of the day's stock of courage and didn't care any more.

'Yes, well it would,' said the houseman. 'You know, it's odd you coming in with this. I don't think I've ever done an ear before.' Thanks a lot, just fucking shut up and get on with it. 'And I did my first nose only a few weeks ago.'

I don't want to hear about it, Duffy thought; just tell me about a nice clean aircrash instead, to keep my mind off things. '*All* 246,000 passengers aboard a pedal cycle of Cockroach Airways were killed this afternoon when . . . '

'I'd never done a nose before. Very nasty; all sort of sliced through as if someone had cut it with a penknife. Mind you, that was the least of his troubles. He'd been in a terrible car smash, and he was, ooh, in a shocking state, but they patched him up, all except for his nose. I suppose it must have been hidden under the oxygen mask or something. Anyway, I got the hang of it eventually. I dare say I will with this. How did you get it?'

'I got it.' Duffy had already told the casualty registrar various lies, so that he wouldn't think it was a criminal injury and feel obliged to ring the police. Something about an ear-ring catching in a fence as he was running along. No, he didn't have the ring for the registrar to examine. He didn't have his stud either, for that matter.

'You don't have to tell me if you don't want to.' No, of course I don't. Duffy felt tired. Still, who gives a stuff one way or the other.

'I wear a stud in it. Some people who don't like me pulled it out,' he said.

'Oh God,' said the houseman, and carried on poking with a needle that felt the size of an oar. 'Well, I think we should all stick together,' he added, leaning a bit more heavily on Duffy's shoulder. The smell of lavender water recurred. Duffy smiled very faintly to himself.

'I think I'm feeling just a bit tired tonight,' he said.

'Did they do something to the other as well?' asked the houseman. 'There's a bruise coming up.'

Duffy felt tired, but it wasn't depressed-tired, so he didn't let it count. His ear throbbed. The houseman had wrapped the bottom half of it tenderly in cotton wool and gauze and plastered it down. Duffy glanced in the mirror and thought he looked like Van Gogh.

He drove back to his flat in Acton and turned round in two minutes. All he needed was his key and his notebook. Then he started back towards Heathrow. He normally made a bit on petrol, but he doubted he would on this job: too much town driving, too much stop-and-start, and then full pelt down the motorway. He was usually late getting up in the mornings, and a steady, petrol-hoarding forty-five became out of the question. Tomorrow he could dawdle, though. Tomorrow he could be as late as he fancied. He could cheek Mrs Boseley as well if he wanted. Might as well be sacked for a wolf . . .

He reached the shed and let himself in with the key as softly as possible, just in case Gleeson was Black-and-Deckering his way through a few more recalcitrant employees. It was all quiet. He neutered the alarm system and padded across to Mrs Boseley's eyrie. Inside, he looked for traces of what had happened only hours before. Was that a drop of blood on the carpet, or just an oil stain? It didn't make any difference. 'Mrs Boseley, we have reason to believe that there is a spot of blood on your carpet.' 'Yes, several of the men keep coming to me with nose bleeds.' Or whatever. The Highland stag gazed benignly down from the National Trust calendar. Duffy flicked it a V-sign.

He found the invoice file where it had been last time he looked. He found the file of forthcoming shipments underneath it. He spent some time copying into his notebook. Then he wandered round the shed, occasionally kicking at hessian-wrapped cases, on the principle expounded by Willett. But only cardboard answered him, never metal. He searched out various shipments and peered at the documentation tags on them. Then he went home, and straight to bed. Fuck it, he thought, I don't like sleeping on my right side.

7

Duffy slept late and got up slowly. His ear didn't feel too good. He rescued some muesli that had been trying to escape from its triple straightjacket of polythene bags, and chewed his way through it without real enthusiasm. He never trusted muesli to be what it said it was. He couldn't believe there weren't jokers in the muesli factories who occasionally slung in a box of sawdust, or a bagful of wood-shavings, or a sack of hedge-clippings, just to see if anyone noticed the difference. They wouldn't, of course. The worse it tasted, the better it was for you: that's what everyone believed.

At ten o'clock he went to the telephone and dialled Carol. She came sleepily to answer it: she'd been on the old shit shift again, six till two in the morning. Yes, she'd love to come round that evening. Anything special? Were they going out? That was a joke, even though she never said it as one. They never went out. Or rather, to be more precise, he never took her out. What did you do last night, Carol? Oh, Duffy didn't take me out again, that's what we did. Her girl friends smiled, because she looked a bit embarrassed. That Duffy, they thought, a real terror in the sack, *we* can tell. We know what *she* means by staying in.

But of course, it wasn't like that. They stayed in, and Duffy cooked her dinner while she teased him about how he always scrubbed the vegetables clean enough for a moon shot; about how the food was trying to escape, and how the knife gave a better reflection than her make-up mirror. They pottered around each other like an old couple. And, contrary to what her girl friends thought, they didn't go to bed together – also like an old couple. They watched television, and chatted, and sometimes, but not necessarily, Carol would drop her watch in the Tupperware box and cuddle up to him for the night. She'd stopped expecting anything to happen. Well, it happened elsewhere; and it was surprising how, after a while of not expecting it, you really didn't mind. You even gave up quietly trying to rub yourself against him. You suspected he didn't like it anyway – brought back too many memories.

Next, Duffy called Willett and asked if he could drop by after work. He had a questionnaire in response to the one old Willett had given him the other day. There was a chuckle of assent. Then he rang a new number, one from his notebook.

'Could I speak to Mr Dalby?'

'I'm afraid Mr Dalby's not available at the moment, sir.' No: probably a bit early. All that late-night pounding up and down Dude's, making sure the corks and the cocks are popping off regularly: it must take it out of a fellow.

'When would be a good time to ring?'

'Well, you could try about eleven.'

'Fine.' That would also make him nice and late for Mrs Boseley; help her pretend to work up a fine head of steam. At eleven o'clock he rang again.

'Mr Dalby in?'

'I'll just see. Who's calling?'

'Oh, just say it's Lord Brown's assistant.'

'Just a moment, sir . . . Putting you through.' They always did, Duffy reflected.

'Hallo, Dalby here.' A precise voice, with neutral intonation, ready to switch to bossy or deferential as the occasion demanded.

'Good morning, Mr Dalby, it's Jeffrey Marcus here, Lord Brown's assistant.' Duffy could do a perfectly unstreet voice if he wanted to. 'It's a private matter, actually, not to do with Lord Brown.'

'Yes.'

'I've been talking to Christopher, and he tells me you're doing business again.'

'Christopher . . . ?' Dalby sounded puzzled, as well he might.

'I know him as Christopher, he's used that to me for a couple of years, but I daresay he uses another one for you. No flies on Christopher.'

'If you say not . . . '

'So if you're doing business again, I'd like to come and see you this evening.'

'Can you be more specific?'

'I don't think that would be wise, do you? Not on this line . . .'

'Oh, I suppose not . . . '

'Shall we say nine o'clock, Mr Dalby? And I'll come to the front door, shall I?' Duffy hoped he'd say, No, not the front door, and give him an alternative, but his confident, almost hectoring tone with Dalby had clearly worked too well.

'Yes, nine o'clock, yes, all right, Mr Marcus, well I'll expect you then.'

At least that had gone smoothly. Duffy regarded the success of the call as moral payment for the damage to his ear; that's to say, the first, extremely small down-payment. As long as the rest of it went as smoothly. As long as he could continue to sweet-talk Dalby in person; as long as Willett came up with the right answers; as long as Mrs Boseley stuck to her agreement and didn't have a frame-up and a copper waiting at the door for him when he turned up to work; as long as plan A – which involved tidiness, intelligence, acuteness and an enormous amount of luck – worked. And if it didn't, he'd have to fall back on plan B, which involved being really rather nasty, cutting a few legal corners, and relying on only a fairly enormous amount of luck.

Duffy ticked off his rosary to himself as he drove slowly to work in the late morning; he felt it wouldn't be good for the van today to exceed forty-five, and dawdled along the M4, tugged at occasionally by the slipstream of airport buses as they swooshed past. The rosary went: fresh flowers, joss-sticks, tinned lychees, pistachio nuts, fresh clams, miscellaneous. Dalby must own a restaurant somewhere as well. He ticked them off, turned them over in his mind, went through them again, forwards, then backwards. It would have to be 'miscellaneous'. His morale sank a bit at the thought. But maybe Willett would tell him differently.

Looking back on the previous evening, Duffy shook his head at himself for the remark about all men having a slice of gay in them. Especially to someone like Gleeson, the inside of whose locker door was a papier mâché of Page Three girls several centimetres thick. And he'd kept his tongue under such good control up till then. It was the sort of remark you might toss at someone offensive you met at a party who was already quite sozzled and had a caliper on his leg, but not at a muscular page-fucker who had your pecker in his pocket, or at least your ear in his pincers. Dumb, Duffy, dumb.

But at the same time, behind the sensation of having half his head torn away there had been a thought struggling out, and the thought was quite simple. It went: Gotcha. Gotcha. That final impulse of Gleeson's to pull Duffy's head off may have been simple queer-bashing; but everything before and after was about something else. The fact that Duffy's ear was at risk in the first place told him that it wasn't just about who he was and where he had met Mr Hendrick. The violence came from nerves, from jumpiness, from a willingness if necessary to wipe out the whole freight shed if that's what it took to get what they wanted; a willingness haunted by a fear that if they did, this might blow it all. Which was why – though Duffy's tail was in any case fairly well covered – they wanted to believe him. They desperately wanted him to be no more than what he had confessed to being when he cracked.

And this jumpiness, coupled with their keenness to sack him on the spot, made Duffy convinced something was going to happen pretty soon; that some shipment or other was on its way. That's why they had been so thrown when the new theft occurred and that's why they wanted to believe Duffy's rather thin, hopeful assurance that he'd fix Casey for them before the end of the week. *They* had no evidence on Casey, or even any knowledge of Duffy's competence; but their worry made them believe they had both.

So Duffy wasn't surprised when Mrs Boseley played her part as arranged. As he was stripping off his jeans top at his locker, Tan was suddenly beside him.

'Missus Bosey see you now soon.'

'Thanks, Tan, I'll think it over.'

'No, now, soon soon, she say.'

'O.K. Tan, O.K.' He stretched self-indulgently, putting on an act for Tan. 'That woman gives me a real pain in the melon, I don't mind telling you.'

' . . . ? You cut yourself?'

'Yeah, I cut myself. Ear today, gone tomorrow. Oh, forget it.'

Tan looked mystified, as well he might, by the different Duffy that had turned up today. This new man slouched across from the lockers to the raised office, pushed open the door and stood just inside it. Both he and Mrs Boseley kept their voices raised so that anyone hanging around could hear.

'You wanted to see me?'

'Yes. Sit down, Duffy.'

'I'm happy here.'

'You're late.'

'So?'

'Don't you *so* me, Duffy, I demand an explanation. Other men have had to do your work until you decided to show up.'

'Well, that makes a change. Normally I get their shitty jobs to do all day. Now they're doing their own for a change.'

'If you're not happy in your work you'd better find another

job. I can't say you'll be missed here.' They were shouting at each other quite loudly by now; out of the corner of his eye Duffy could see a baffled Casey, plus one of the drivers, looking up at them.

'I wouldn't mind it if there weren't so many *cunts* around this place.' That should be enough, he thought; however much they dislike Mrs Boseley, they'll see that as a sackable offence.

'You're fired.'

'It can't be soon enough as far as I'm concerned.'

'I want you out in a week. Now get back to your work.'

Duffy kicked at the glass door but found that it was wisely reinforced. As he clattered down the steps he shouted over his shoulder, 'Needs a cowing union, this place.'

Though the bravado was fake, it still somehow infected Duffy. He was playing a game with Mrs Boseley, but he still enjoyed bawling her out in front of the shed. He sat in his dunce's corner feeling quite chipper for most of the morning. And when the dinner whistle went a surprising thing happened. Casey lolloped across to him and punched him on the bicep.

'Canteen,' he said, clearly and loudly. Duffy felt like an animal experimenter who had finally taught one of his charges to imitate the sound of the human voice. The effort, however, took a lot out of Casey, and over his double spaghetti hoops and chips he slumped back into his normal taciturnity. When he threw his spoon down after his double plum duff and exhaled loudly, Duffy thought he might pick the conversation up.

'What a day,' he said. 'Nearly slice me ear off shaving, and then get the boot.'

Casey frowned. He appeared to be thinking for a very long time. Then he said, in a tone of extreme confidentiality, 'Like the way you call 'er cun'. Herher.'

Duffy felt almost moved. Casey was, he guessed, expressing a sort of affection for him. What a pity it had taken so long. What a pity they would only be lunching together for another week or so. What a pity Duffy might have to dump Casey in the shit.

After work he rolled along to Terminal One again, to the Apple Tree Buffet. The same air of mass panic reigned, as ever, only transferred to a new set of damp-palmed passengers.

'A couple of factual points,' he said to Willett, 'and a quiz.'

'Fire away.'

'Factual point one. You find a bag of heroin. Doesn't matter where, Chinaman's bum or wherever. What happens?'

'Well I guess we'd pull it out first.'

'And then?'

'We do a field test on it. We've got a little kit. Just to make sure it isn't contraband salt or something they're trying to smuggle in.'

'And that tells you what it is.'

'More or less, yes. Then we send it to the Government Chemist. Under seal, of course, so that the courier doesn't get too merry. They analyse it for us and report back.'

'And what can they tell?'

'Well, they tell you what it is. They tell you how old it is. They tell you where it comes from. That's one of the more satisfactory sides of it all: the analysis is incredibly precise. It's helped, of course, by the fact that no two batches will ever be the same – unless they're made at the same time in the same factory, of course. And as so much of it is cottage-industry work, well, that's a help. I mean, you wouldn't get two batches of heroin the same any more than you'd get a pair of salt-glaze plates coming out the same.'

Duffy didn't need the comparison. For a start, he didn't understand it.

'And if . . . supposing, say, the courier had a bag – say there were two bags, and they got split up, on the plane or wherever, and they were found some distance apart: would the Chemist be able to prove that they were part of the same batch?'

'Oh yes. No problem. It's often the only evidence we've got

that, say, a couple of dealers are connected. But it's very strong evidence.'

'Hmmm. Good. End of part one. Ready for the quiz?'

'Yes.'

'You are a smuggler.' It seemed only tit for tat: Willett had made *him* play a customs officer. 'You have a certain amount of heroin.'

'What form?'

'What do you mean, what form?'

'Well, it's not just powder necessarily. It can be dissolved into a solution, made into paste. Can I do what I like with it?'

'You can do what you like with it. All you have to do is get it through customs – through me. I'm a keen but relatively new assistant officer.'

'No problem.'

'No, you have to do it in one of six ways. You're freighting in six sorts of cargo, and it has to go in one – or perhaps more than one – of them. Ready?'

'Ready.'

'O.K., here's your starter for ten. Pistachio nuts.'

'Are those those little green buggers?'

'Yuh.'

'Sort of half-open but you still break your fingernails on them? Some of them are open and you break your fingernails; some of them are closed and you break your teeth?'

'Yuh.'

'Shouldn't be too difficult.' Willett thought for a minute or so. 'Powder form. Break out some of the half-open ones, fill the shell with stuff, glue the two halves shut.'

'What, individually?'

'Sure. You get enough in each to buy a car with. Once it's cut for street selling. And they're sort of dusted over with salt or something, aren't they?'

'Yes.'

'That'll help. No trouble. We've got them through. Next?'

'Joss-sticks.'

'Hmmm. How do they come?'

'Oh, not sure. Let's say, packets of, what, twenty, thirty? Few dozen packets to the case.'

'What sort of packet? Paper?'

'Yeah, O.K. Well, cardboard box, say, and a paper label.'

'That's trickier. Couldn't exactly drill the sticks. Making it into sticks and painting it? No. No – it'll have to be the packaging. Not too difficult, but long and messy as the boxes aren't that big, but O.K. Soak the labels off, make the heroin up into paste, and paste them back on. That should get through you.'

'Tinned lychees.'

'Tins. Can be good, can be bad. Depends entirely on the state of your ancillary technology. If you have a little canning factory on the side, of course, no problem. Three ways, I suppose. You could use the paste method on the label. Or you could use a draining method: that's to say, you take off the label, bore a tiny hole in the can – no, I suppose you'd need two, wouldn't you, one for the air – and pour off the liquid. Then you refill with dissolved heroin – just bung it in with a syringe. Stick the label back on and Bob's your uncle.'

'What about the lychees?'

'Oh, you just leave them in. Unless, of course, heroin and lychees set up some sort of chemical reaction I don't know about. But dissolved heroin's very popular. You've no idea how many bottles of soya sauce and Chinese wine we've opened to no very good effect.'

'And the third way?'

'Well, what's easiest for the man at the other end is if you can interfere at the canning stage – either that or have the technology to take out the can lid and then reweld it. Then you just dump the bag of heroin inside, fill up with a few lychees until you get exactly the same weight as all the other cans, and reseal it.'

'How does the person at the other end recognise the can?'

'No trouble. Simple code – say, a couple of tiny pinpricks in the label, in prearranged places. Unless we get tipped off – or unless we open every single can that comes through – there's no possibility of our spotting it. And if we tried opening every can that came through whose label wasn't in absolutely perfect nick – well, we'd have to have a whole separate department, wouldn't we?'

'Fresh flowers.'

'What sort?'

'Er – various.'

'In that case – various possibilities. If they're exotic, you know, big fleshy stems, you could work a thin plastic straw of stuff up the inside of the stalks. You could use the packaging in the same way as with the joss-sticks – paste form. You could – though this would depend on where they were coming from and how long they were taking – use cloth or maybe cotton wool soaked in heroin solution, to look as if they were keeping the flowers damp. It's a bit of a long shot, but that sort of thing has been done. Oh, and there's another clever thing with flowers I heard once. Not in this country, though. They got a local artist – must have been a very skilled fellow – to paint on to bits of paper what looked like the bottoms of the inside of flowers: you know, the sort with big bells to them. Then they stuck these inside and had what was in effect a false-bottomed flower; room for a fair amount of stuff between the two bottoms.'

'Like a suitcase.'

'Exactly. Bloody clever. You wouldn't look there, would you?'

'No. Fresh clams.'

'I don't really know what they look like; I'd have to have a gander at them first. If they're closed up – or if some of them are – you can just use the pistachio nut principle. If they're open: bit trickier, might have to use the shells in some way. Well, if that's too hard I'd just go for the packaging.'

'Uh-huh. And last of the six: Miscellaneous.'

'What do you mean?'

'Well, that's what it says on the documentation.'

'Bits of everything?'

'I suppose so.'

'Well, then it's my birthday, isn't it – looking at it one way. I mean, if you've got a case with a dozen different things in, I'll find you a dozen different methods, and then I'll pick the best, and you'd never find it, except of course that you might.'

'Why might I?'

'Because you'd look quite closely at something coming through called Miscellaneous. It seems a bit too likely, given that you've got any suspicions at all. It's just the method some not-too-professional guy might use for a big one-off shipment.'

'Uh-huh. So which of the six would you use?'

'Well, don't forget I might well come up with better methods for each of them, given a bit of time. I mean, that's what it's all about. Those guys out there spend months, sometimes years, thinking up something which we either spot or don't spot in seconds or minutes. It's not very good odds. And they're always changing. As soon as any method is busted – and often, if they're smart, before – they move on; the clever guys never use the same system once it's been blown, wherever in the world.'

'So which would you use?'

'I don't like the clams, though I'd have to have another think about them. I don't like the joss-sticks because that might make some keen young assistant officer start thinking of opium dens or whatever. As I said, I don't like Miscellaneous. I'd go for the nuts, the tins, or the flowers. At that stage it depends on your personality as much as anything. Flowers if I were a bit more fanciful than I am; tins if I had the technology; nuts if I had the patience. But don't misunderstand me – I'd get past you. I'd get past *you*, anyway.'

Duffy pondered. Was that a quiet appeal? A don't-do-anything-on-your-own-lad bit of advice? Possibly. If you were Willett, you wouldn't enjoy the thought of amateurs trying to play customs men; you'd expect a tip-off, an appeal to the professionals. Fair enough – except that Duffy had no details: no shipment time, no specific goods to watch, just a hypothesis. Officer, open that hypothesis at once. Just as I thought: a false bottom.

He decided to half-respond to Willett's appeal.

'If I got on to anything . . . '

'Yes?'

'How far does your authority run?'

'Everywhere.'

'You mean, outside the bonded area? As far as Hendrick Freight?'

'No, I mean everywhere. You don't get an amnesty just because you've got something through the customs. If goods are prohibited or dutiable they stay that way. We'll come looking you up wherever you are.'

'Ah. Well, in that case I don't think I'll try. I'll dump my stuff overboard from the cross-Channel ferry.'

Willett's creased face crinkled up a little more.

'Well, watch the currents is my advice.'

' . . . ?'

'Case a few years ago. Some fellow in a private aircraft got cold feet. Flying in with a nice bale of stuff that wasn't exactly feed for his cattle. Hay content pretty low, as you might say. Anyway, got cold feet, dumped all the stuff in the Channel. Landed, went home, felt a lot poorer but a lot more relieved. Few days went by, and the tide washes up this great bundle of dope on the Dorset coast. Somebody's birthday, the old farmer thinks, and smokes a fair bit of it before he realises it's that funny stuff they're always going on about in the papers. Calls us in, we trace it, and do the pilot for illegally importing it.'

That seemed a bit thick to Duffy. He grunted, and went on.

'This is factual point number two, by the way. If I got on to anything, I could give you a call?'

'You'd be mad not to.' Willett was proud of his profession, proud of the way Heathrow had moved in recent years. It had got a lot tighter. Of course, this meant that the clever guys were trying elsewhere – Luton, for instance, and soft, package-tour airports where bandits swirl through the green channel in a bustle of tired perms and duty-free Tia Maria. But even so, that was grounds for local pride.

'I could be . . . quite general, could I?'

'Oh yes – often we just get tips along the lines of: Jamaica, some time this month. But it gives us more of a chance.'

'Or if . . . I was very specific?' Duffy, as always, was keen to cover his tail.

'Second locker along, top shelf. We wouldn't object to that, mate.'

'And what about my position if I rang you – or someone else if you're not on duty?'

'Well, if I'm not around, ask for Dickie Mallett: first-rate chap. As for you: I couldn't be absolutely positive, I'm not a lawyer. But I'd say that you'd have at least as much immunity as was necessary for us to make sure we'd get the information.'

That sounded nice and legal: in other words, muddled and incomprehensible. Duffy tried again.

'If I rang you up, and didn't say who I was, just said, "I'm an interested member of the public" – say I said exactly that, but you knew I was me, and then I tipped you off. Would you have to pass on that you knew it was me?'

Willett realised that this wasn't part of the quiz (not that the quiz hadn't been for real, he reflected); he was being tested. He gave it a few moments' thought.

'I think I'd think,' he replied eventually, 'that if you used that formula, you'd be stating your terms, and I'd have to accept them. I'd also argue, for form's sake, that if I didn't guard your identity the first time round, then there wouldn't be any hope of there being a second time round.'

Duffy smiled. He didn't think there was much chance of a second time – he didn't much want to work around airports again. But he'd got his deal.

He'd got his deal, but Willett had also blown Plan A for him.

133

Well, it had been naïve of him in the first place to expect that his friend would just reply, No, No, No, No, No and then Yes, it'll be in the third clam on the right in the next delivery but one. That was stupid; but he'd gone along with half-believing it because he wasn't too keen on Plan B. Then he touched the bit of his left ear that was allowed to protrude from the houseman's tender swaddling, and he got a bit less unkeen on Plan B.

Christ, he'd double-booked Carol. Should he call her, or pretend that the Dalby business had cropped up subsequently? Well, in a way it had, he supposed. Think about it later, he said to himself. There are a couple of calls to be made first, and a couple of connections. One of which meant very bad news for somebody.

As he dialled Geoff Bell's number, he worked at his opening gag. Bell was a friend whom Duffy used occasionally for help on the technical side of things. He could bug a phone merely by scowling at it; he could photograph through brick walls. Duffy had once foolishly bet him a fiver that he couldn't get a photo of him, Duffy, in his underpants, within a week. Duffy went around for two days being extremely careful where he dropped his trousers. He needn't have bothered. On the third day in the post he got a blurred, grainy but unambiguous snap of himself and a friend from the Alligator. In a very post-underpants condition. Bell's covering note read: 'I'll keep trying for one with the underpants if you like.' As there were four days to go on the bet, Duffy didn't rate his chances and paid up.

Bell recorded every incoming telephone call, so Duffy always began his in satirical vein:

'Ah, Geoff,' he said when he got through, 'this is AQ35B about the Tripoli connection. If we put the plastic under the second oil-well rather than the third, then we could use the lighter detonators and run the fuse straight across the Med to Malta.'

'Duffy, how are you? Haven't heard from you for ages. Not

since that wipe-job you gave me.' Sometimes Duffy despaired of Bell. What was an introductory game to Duffy was an entirely serious test to Bell.

'Got something rather tricky coming up, Geoff, wondered if you could help.'

Duffy had something rather simple coming up, as a matter of fact; it was just that Bell didn't get excited by simple jobs.

'Are you free tomorrow night?'

'Yes.'

'I'm going to need a body-recorder some time around six, and then a bit later, not sure when, I'm going to need three copies done and taken to three different addresses as quickly as possible. I'll probably be dodging bullets at the time,' he added melodramatically.

'Well don't use a police vest, you can shoot Rice Krispies through them. If you've got the right weapon, of course. Like a pea-shooter.'

'What about the taping?' Trust Geoff to seize the inessential first.

'Well, we'll do it in series, so that you get the same quality on each instead of a slightly deteriorating one, and . . . ' Geoff went on for some time, but Duffy didn't listen: Bell was talking to himself really.

The second call he made was to Christine, a nurse he'd met a few months ago. Physically, she overlapped with Carol a bit too much for Duffy to feel it was O.K. to fancy her; so he just took her out a few times, now and then, feeling a bit bad towards Carol when he did so. She, in turn, was quite pleased that Duffy wasn't a doctor, and that gynecological examination wasn't going to be called for before the first half can of beer had been downed, the first packet of crisps finished. Duffy never asked for that. Indeed, this time, on the phone, it was the first time he'd asked for anything. He said he needed what he needed for some amateur dramatics; well, actually, for a comic sketch he was doing with some friends at a pub. Could she come? No, he'd be embarrassed in front of her, he'd freeze; but if he did it again, sure she could come. Could she borrow one for him? Christine said it was strictly against hospital regulations; but they were always throwing them away, and if it wasn't for use . . . No, said Duffy, but it must look as if it could be used – there might be some doctors in the audience who'd complain if it didn't have the right end on it. And he could pick it up tomorrow? Lovely.

At 7.30 Carol arrived in her Mini.

'What's it to be tonight, Duffy? Cheese on toast, or grilled bread with a cheese topping? Christ, what have you done to your ear?'

'Shaving. It's all right, doesn't hurt. I'm having moussaka and chips, and you can have whatever's on the menu under four quid.'

'Duffy . . . ' and there was a curve of surprise and delight in her tone as she drew out the name, 'we're not going out, are we?'

'All right.'

'You should have told me, I'd have changed.'

Duffy looked embarrassed. Carol thought this was because he felt guilty about how long it had been since he'd last taken her out. But he went on looking embarrassed.

'Duffy,' she said sternly, 'what's the catch?'

'Nnn?'

'What's the catch, Duffy?'

'Eh? No catch.' But she could tell there was. 'I've got to see a man on the way, that's all.'

'Duffy, you are a bugger.' He gave her a wary grin.

'I know.'

At 8.30 they left and drove slowly into town. When Carol saw the direction in which they were going, she turned to him and said, 'You're not taking me to work, are you, Duffy? I mean, I don't need to clock in till tomorrow morning.' That made him look even more embarrassed.

They drove much closer to Dude's this time, and parked about thirty yards short of it.

'That's where I'm going,' he said, pointing down the street. 'Shan't be long.'

'You *are* a dirty bugger, Duffy. If I see one of my mates tootling past, I'll send them in just to see you aren't up to any monkey business.' But she didn't really mean it. If Duffy wanted to spend his money in posh massage parlours, then that was up to him. She couldn't disapprove. And at least it was with women.

There was a different hat-check girl tonight. Blonde, and with breasts . . . no, Duffy didn't really want to look at them. There was something about this place that made you feel a lot dirtier, and at the same time a lot less interested. Fifteen pairs of breasts ought to be fifteen times more exciting than one pair; but it didn't work like that. Even in the booth with the girl he hadn't really felt much interest in her breasts, because they didn't seem to be hers: they seemed to be part of the club's fixtures and fittings. Clipped on, and then put back on the shelf at two in the morning when the last puffing punter was given his hat and eased out into the street.

'Do you charge?' he said to the girl, suddenly curious.

'Twenty pounds, sir . . . '

'No – no, I mean for leaving your hat.'

'Your hat? Not many gentlemen have them nowadays,' she said.

'Or your coat. Does the cloakroom charge, is all I'm saying.'

'Oh *no* sir, certainly not.' She seemed quite offended. 'Though of course, you can always tip us,' she added. Of course. Always. The pound change from the price of a single whisky – that would be about right. He felt irritated.

'Appointment with Mr Dalby,' he said, rather curtly.

'Oh, well, sir, I'll have to see if he's free.'

'The name's Marcus.'

'Marcus what?'

'*Mister* Marcus.' Duffy realised he had picked himself a pseudonym made out of two Christian names. Like Eric Leonard. A name that wasn't serious.

'Oh, of course.' The girl seemed abashed. Duffy felt like a bully. That was probably just as well; he had to get into the right mood for bluffing Dalby.

He rather hoped he wouldn't be recognised by the girl with the northern accent and the breasts which were located in the middle of the graph. Still, how long did a punter stay in their minds – ten minutes? And besides, he looked different now; instead of Fifties revival and tincture of mothballs, he was all velved up. Blue jacket, blue trousers – a close enough match in this light to pass for a suit – boots, and a mauve shirt open at the neck. Did he look like Lord Brown's assistant? Did he look like a dealer? Well, it was up to him to turn those equations round: he didn't have to look like either of them if he made both of *them* look like *him*.

He gave a hooded glance at the girl-strewn bar as he was led towards the stairs. The same smell of joss-sticks. Just as dark downstairs. The booths with their slatted half-doors; the hands clamped to the breasts as if with superglue; the wet bottles; the fresh flowers; the artificial tones of hostess conversation; the balding husbands with good suits and bad consciences.

'Mr Marcus, a pleasure.' Dalby had come out of his office to greet him, and paused briefly to inspect the scene below. You couldn't actually hear the peeling-off of ten pound notes; but you could imagine it well enough from here, Duffy thought.

At first Dalby's office seemed floodlit, but it was only the contrast. Duffy sat in a high-backed tapestry-work chair across the desk from the club owner. He took his time, and looked around the office for a few seconds as if he were thinking of buying it. He took in the standard lamp, the sofa, the small bookcase, the series of large prints round the walls. They looked like early woodcuts which, for modern reproduction, had been enlarged about twenty times; they showed pastoral scenes. The one behind Dalby's head depicted a large tethered horse, a cow, a sheep, and a couple of thatched cottages. Centuries, and worlds away from Dude's. Unless, of course, the tethered horse belonged to Ye Olde Opium Dealer who had called in at one of the cottages to make a connection.

Dalby coughed, and Duffy permitted his eye to return slowly to the cougher. Dalby was watching him rather damply from behind his little round gold spectacles. Duffy decided that he momentarily had the initiative; and this was the way it was going to stay. If you bluff, bluff big, he thought, and bluff aggressive. Also, as a sign of confidence, leave out the shifty, ambiguous half-language of the trade. Dalby looked the sort of dealer who lived by circumlocution and might fret at straight talk.

'The room's clean,' said Duffy sharply, in his unstreet voice. It was an affirmation rather than a question.

'Oh yes.'

Duffy looked across at the open door past Dalby's left shoulder, which led, presumably, to his bedroom, and the bathroom with the post-coital tub. He let his held glance act as his second question.

'We're quite alone,' Dalby assured him.

Duffy then talked quickly and confidently, as befitted Lord Brown's assistant.

'I've got two hundredweight of grass coming in fairly soon, though from what I hear of you you won't be very interested in that. Can't say I blame you, it's such a long-winded drug, isn't it; and personally I find cigarettes a disgusting habit, though I cast no aspersions. I've got a moderate amount of coke coming in next week or so. And I've just had some excellent Chinese Number Three which is being cut at the moment. That's my shopping list. Why you? Because I need money now for my next import, which is quite substantial. I wouldn't go outside otherwise. I hear you're reliable and honest – that's what I hear, anyway – and if you don't mind my saying so, you're British, which makes a nice change. Of course, if you aren't – I don't mean British, I mean the other things – I don't advise you to deal with me.'

Duffy gazed at Dalby impassively while awaiting his reply.

'Er . . . um . . . um . . . ' He seemed thrown by such direct-ness. Thrown enough, Duffy hoped, not to go into the ques-tion of who the invented 'Christopher' might be.

' . . . er . . . price?' he said eventually, as if forcing himself to use a dirty word.

'The coke or the smack?'

'The er . . . former.' (Which meant that he was interested only in the former; or that he had his own supplies of the latter on the way?)

'Sliding scale, depends on purity. I'll have to wait and see when it arrives. My rates are middle-of-the-market. Twenty to thirty a gram. You want some?'

'Er . . . yeees.'

'Good, fine,' said Duffy, as if he had another few calls to make that evening. He got up and extended his palm.

'It's all on the handshake,' he said. Dalby took it as if it were an honour. 'Oh, by the way, I seemed to disturb some of your customers on the way in. Is there another way out?'

'Oh yes, this way.' He took Duffy out of the office, along a corridor away from the booths, down a passage and out through a back door. No alarm system, simple door: Duffy was laugh-ing. Dalby held the door open; Duffy nodded, but without looking at him, and strode out into the dark. That had been a strain.

'Did they do wonderful things to you?' Carol asked as he slid into the van. It was a half-serious tease. It was also near a dangerous subject.

'Wonderful,' replied Duffy in a dreamy voice. 'Only costs fifty-four pounds.'

'Will you take me some time?' she asked. But Duffy only chuckled to himself.

Later, as they sat over kebabs and tried to make themselves heard above the Zorba music, he said, 'I might let you go on your own.'

'Where?'

'That place – Dude's.'

'What do you mean?'

'Well, I was just wondering who you might be having dinner with tonight.' Carol looked puzzled. Duffy winked.

'I'll pay, of course, but if you take the bill, then you can charge it, can't you, if it works out?'

She leaned over and tapped her knuckles on the top of his head, as if to restore order in there.

'I mean, it's a way of repaying you really, isn't it?'

Sometimes, she didn't understand him at all, even when she looked back on it later.

'Your kebab's getting cold.' Why was he smiling at her like that?

He drove her back to Acton, since her car was there already, and as it was late she decided to stay the night. They went into the flat and Duffy turned all the lights on, even though they were going straight to bed. He always liked to have a last look round. It made him feel more secure about going to sleep.

'Duffy,' she said to him as she cuddled into his back.

'Mnnn.' He was almost asleep.

'I like that velvet suit.'

'Mnnn.'

'Pity it doesn't match.'

8

The next day, when he arrived for work, Duffy was again greeted by a punch on the bicep from Casey, and a chortle of 'Cun''. This flutter of affection from the Tattooed Man touched Duffy, and he began to wonder if he could unfix Casey. If he didn't have to fix him, if he could leave all the thieving with McKay where it truly belonged, then that would square him with Hendrick. And if he unfixed Casey, then that would also be another promise broken towards Mrs Boseley, and that couldn't be bad. It might be just worth a try, as long as it didn't put him out too much.

At lunchtime he telephoned the hifi villains. If they had any sense, they wouldn't have rushed straight round to their nearest middleman with the stuff; they'd wait a few days just to see if there wasn't going to be any follow-up. He got the driver who liked the oil patches. Duffy's voice was tuned to its streetiest.

'It's Duffy 'ere, from 'endrick, 'eafrow. 'Bout that case of sparks I frew in by mistake the uvver day. O.K. if I come rahnd this evening?'

'What, mate?'

'Case of sparks you got wiv yer hifi. I loaded for yer. Frew 'em in by mistake.'

'Sparks?'

'Ligh'ers, you know, snout ligh'ers. Frew in a case. Gotta ge'hem back or get the cowing sack.'

'Can't say I remember any, mate.'

'Awri', well, you prob'ly didn' unload them. Prob'ly still sittin' wivver hifi. But we go'hem booked aht t'ya, see?'

'I'll just go and check, old cock.'

'Awri'.'

He was away several minutes, and Duffy was afraid of running out of 10p pieces before he returned. He sounded displeased.

'We found them, mate, they were in with some tape-decks.'

'Fanks, oh fanks a lot, you saved my skin.'

'Well, I'm afraid one or two of them are missing. Someone seems to have been helping himself round here.' The hifi villain's pound of flesh, Duffy thought.

'Lock 'em up till I get rahnd, willya? And fanks. You saved my skin.'

'Any time.'

He didn't sound as if he meant it.

It was going to be a busy evening, he could see that, so he decided to start early. Skipping off work at half four would irritate Mrs Boseley a great deal, which was of course an end in itself, but it would also enable him to get to the hifi villains in Ealing before they closed.

He picked up 140 of the original gross of lighters which he had switched, and drove home. Then he went to the nurses' hostel and collected a small item from Christine. Home again, he packed a holdall with everything he thought he'd need and set off for Geoff's flat. As he rang the bell, he pulled down his zip, and let his trousers gape. He did this every time he called on Bell.

'Do your flies up, Duffy,' said the entryphone. Duffy smiled. He'd never been able to spot the camera. Most people liked to let you know you were being spied on, through the fish-eye lens in the door, or the not-so-hidden camera; it gave them a sense of power as well as of security. Bell got his pleasure from knowing that you didn't know you were being examined.

'Armpit, groin or back?' was his greeting. Duffy groaned to

himself. It was always like this. He tried to show as much interest as possible in Bell's techniques, but the fellow did exaggerate. There were fifteen miniature tape recorders laid out for inspection on the work bench. Duffy imagined the arguments about their respective merits that would doubtless ensue: arguments not between Duffy and Bell, but between Bell and Bell.

'Does it matter?'

'Of course it matters. It's the first question. Where do you want the mike, where do you want the recorder?'

'I don't know. Are there any factors that make any difference?'

'Course there are, Duffy. Who are you taping? And where? I don't want to be told, of course, I just want to be told enough. How long do you want to record for? How far away will your friend be? Will you both be stationary? Is there going to be any background noise? Will you be able to slip away and change the tape?'

'I see,' said Duffy, but Bell had only paused for breath.

'Will you want to change your clothes? Is it as important to record you as it is your friend? Will there be any third parties? And then, of course, there are the physical matters.'

'What do you mean?'

'Is anyone likely to try and kick you in the balls? Or punch you in the back? Will you want to hit anyone while you're recording? Or before you're recording? Will you want a stop on the recorder so that you can pause the tape, hit someone, and then go back to recording?'

'You don't think I'm very nice, do you, Geoff?'

'What? What do you mean?' Bell, Duffy realised from his surprised expression, had been talking from a purely technical angle. Hitting someone, as far as he was concerned, was merely a factor which might interfere with sound quality.

Duffy began to outline what he needed. He'd estimated that the visit might take forty minutes; in the event it took two hours. He emerged feeling as if he'd just had all his ribs bandaged at Uxbridge Hospital. A recorder the size of a crispbread was plastered into the small of his back; wires ran into each of the pockets of his blouson: switch in the right pocket to start, switch in the left pocket to pause. He'd better remember *that*.

It was dark now as he drove along the M4. All that survived of the mad, self-destructive jumbos were a few twitching lights in the sky; red, green, white. It was their fault if they crashed now, Duffy reflected: going out in the dark like that. It shouldn't be allowed.

At the shed he unloaded the cigarette lighters and dumped them close to his dunce's corner. He'd think up a story for Hendrick later. First, though, he had to get through Plan B. He flicked the top of his left ear and made it throb. That made him feel better about Plan B. He picked his way across to Mrs Boseley's glass office, dumped his holdall beside the desk, sat in her chair, steered his foot well away from the security buzzer, took a deep breath and picked up the phone.

Come on, come on, answer it, you've been in every time I've watched you, don't go out tonight, maybe you're polishing that big Granada of yours in the drive, come on, ah –

'Gleeson, it's Duffy. Yes, Duffy from work, that's right.'

'What the fuck do you want?'

The main thing was, to get it in the right order, not give him anything which would make him ring off before he saw he had no choice but to pick the course of action Duffy was leading him towards.

'I called Mrs Boseley, but her husband said she'd gone to stay with a friend for the night.' Get *that* into his skull for a start.

'Where did you get my number from? Why are you calling?'

'I got your number from a big book which is sitting in front of me called E–K. All right?'

'Why are you calling me?'

'I found some heroin today at the shed.'

'You *what*? Duffy, where are you?'

Duffy let that pass. He paused. He rather felt he had Gleeson's attention for a while.

'At least I thought it might be. So I took a bit of it – you may have noticed I left early – and I showed it to a friend, who said he thought it probably was, and we'd better hand it in or something. I said I'd better ring the people at Hendrick Freight, so I got out the phone book . . . ' He enjoyed spinning it out.

'Where on earth did you find it?'

' . . . and I rang Mr Hendrick.' Pause at that.

'What did he say?' Gleeson didn't sound too secure.

'Oh, he wasn't there, he's out for the evening. Then I rang Mrs Boseley as I said, and she's out for the night, so I thought maybe you'd know what to do.'

'Quite right, Duffy. Let me think.'

Duffy gave him about four seconds' space and then said, 'Shall I call the police?'

'Let's not rush anything, Duffy. Let me think. I mean, we don't want it to look bad for Hendrick Freight.' That set it up nicely.

'I don't care the fuck how bad it looks for Hendrick Freight. What do I owe Hendrick Freight? How much is Hendrick Freight giving me for my fucking ear? I'm going to ring the fucking police.' He let his voice climb towards the hysterical.

'Don't, Duffy,' said Gleeson. 'Stop, let's think it out. No, of course you don't care about the company, why should you? But I don't want to be hasty.'

Duffy reckoned he had him now. He put on a calmer tone.

'Well, *if* you want to think it over, I suppose I could show you where it is. I mean, I've got a key to the shed.' The hook was going into the roof of the mouth: would he notice?

'You what? How?'

'Yeah. Didn't ever use it, but Mr Hendrick gave me one when he hired me.'

'O.K., that's a good idea. It'd be awkward tomorrow with all the other people around. Where are you now?'

'I'm at home, but I can get out there in about half an hour. If I get there before you I'll let myself in and turn on one of the small lights. I shouldn't think it's a good idea to turn them all on.'

'No, quite right. I'll set off straight away now. Oh, and, maybe you could bring that bit of the stuff you took this afternoon. Then we can put it all back together.'

'Of course.'

Duffy put down the phone. Then he took a chair from Mrs Boseley's office and placed it beneath the one light he had turned on, about a third of the way down the shed. Next to the chair he put his holdall, having first extracted a couple of items which he stuffed down the front of his blouson. Then he went over and waited near the side door for Gleeson to arrive. He'd have two advantages: Gleeson wouldn't know quite where he was, and it was very dark in the shed. It was even darker than in Dalby's wankpit. Twenty minutes went by.

'Duffy.' The side door clicked shut and Gleeson stood there blinking into the murk.

'Over here,' said Duffy from about ten yards away. Gleeson walked towards him, and Duffy immediately said, in as peremptory way as possible, 'This way.'

He turned away from Gleeson and set off fast across the shed. That's what it looked like to Gleeson, anyway, who trotted in pursuit. Except that after taking four paces Duffy wheeled round, and, as Gleeson came up to him, punched him extremely hard at the top of the stomach. Gleeson's momentum increased the effect of the punch: he bent half-forward, gasping for breath. Duffy wasn't much of a believer in the left-uppercut, right-cross-to-the-point-of-the-chin school of fighting. If you had hurt someone in a particular place, it always seemed logical to Duffy to hurt them some more in the same place. This time he used his knee. Then he used his fist again.

Gleeson didn't fall over. He just stood there, all gorilla-armed, eyes popping, as if he was in the middle of a heart attack. He barely noticed as Duffy dug into his blouson and handcuffed his wrists. He racked them up tight, the way he used to do with villains he really disapproved of. Then he dug out a length of rope and sat on the floor by Gleeson's feet. He looped the rope round the far foot and pulled it until it was next to its partner, almost toppling Gleeson in the process. Then he tied the ankles together.

Duffy took a while to get his breath back. Gleeson took longer. Duffy gave him time for the heart attack to subside. He wasn't a sadist. Not yet. Then he said,

'Hop.'

Gleeson stared at him, half-scared, half-puzzled. Duffy pointed across the shed at the chair set up under the light.

'Hop. Oh, and by the way, if you feel like shouting, I'll put a gag in your mouth and pour half a pint of Castrol down your nose. All right?'

Gleeson hopped, like a child in a school race. He looked pathetic. He looked as if he'd gone in for the sack race and someone had stolen his sack. Duffy didn't feel sorry for him. He thought he could hold that sentiment at bay for as long as it took. For ever, come to think of it.

Gleeson hopped as far as the chair, looked at Duffy, and sat himself down in it. Duffy got out some more rope and tied him to the chair.

'Right,' he said, 'here are the rules. If I tip you over from this side, you smash the back of your head in. If I push you over from behind, you smash your face in. If you start screaming, I pour Castrol down your nose, O.K.?'

Gleeson could have worked most of that out for himself. But Duffy wanted him to know that their minds were as one. Gleeson nodded. He looked scared. He was right to be.

Duffy pulled over two empty packing-cases and placed them just outside Gleeson's kicking range. He sat down on one, and unpacked his holdall on the other. He did it in an order which, he hoped, would keep Gleeson guessing for as long as possible. First a box of matches. Then a lemon. Then a candle. Then a knife. Then two saucers. Then a small tin of Marvel milk.

Then a plastic bottle. Then a spoon. Then a small polythene bag of white powder. Then an oblong cardboard box. He opened the box and took out a hypodermic. Then he lit the candle. Then he looked at Gleeson. Then he said,

'Right.' And flicked out the match.

'I don't know anything about this,' said Gleeson.

Duffy barely paid attention to him. That's what they all said. Some of them used to say it whimperingly, pathetically, when they'd been caught with their pants messed and the half-dressed child on their knee; some of them said it confidently, aggressively, when they'd been picked off the street outside Fine Fare and thought they'd just cleared the goods through the fence in time, and they knew their fucking rights and Bendy Benson, lawyer to crooks for twenty years, would be round to fix them bail pretty soon.

Gleeson said it midway between these two points. But even if he'd said it at the top end of the scale of confidence, Duffy wouldn't have been perturbed. No Bendy Benson would be popping into Hendrick Freight tonight, with his soiled brief-case and paralysing attacks of fairmindedness. And Duffy wouldn't exactly be fretting about the Judges' Rules. He might even have to trot round the back of Gleeson from time to time and see how he liked *that*.

'I don't know anything about this,' repeated Gleeson, in the sad mumble of a drinker into his beer.

'Gleeson, this isn't going to be complicated,' said Duffy, still not bothering to look at him. 'It may be painful, but it isn't going to be complicated. Oh, one thing first, though.'

He dug into Gleeson's inside jacket pocket, leaning close to his face as he did so but again pretending he wasn't there, and pulled out Gleeson's wallet.

'Fair amount of folding in here. I should be careful where you go, carrying this lot around.' He reached in and took out twenty pounds. 'That's for the stud, Gleeson. I reckon that's what it'll cost. And you're lucky I'm National Health, otherwise it would have burned you a sight more.'

Gleeson falsely discerned a lightening in Duffy's tone.

'I didn't really mean to do it,' he said.

'That makes it worse, not better,' replied Duffy coldly. He walked round the back of the chair, noted where the useful parts of Gleeson's back were, and readjusted him so that the crossbar didn't protect his kidneys too much. While he stood there he flicked the Start switch in the right-hand pocket of his blouson.

'Right. Now you're going to tell me everything you know, from the beginning.' A stab on the Pause button in the left-hand pocket. 'And if you stop, or hesitate, or lie, I'm going to hurt you. And if you scream or shout, you'll get Castrol down your nose.' To indicate that this wasn't a figure of speech, Duffy dug into his holdall and placed a round, one-pint tin of the oil on the packing-case.

'I don't know what you're talking about.'

'You're going to tell me all about the heroin, and Mrs Boseley, and Dalby, and how it comes in, and where it comes from, and who it goes to, and when the next shipment's coming through.' Always ask them more than they're likely to know, that was one of the rules.

'I just work here.'

Duffy walked round the back, flipped the Pause button, punched Gleeson hard in the kidneys, waited, punched him once more, and started recording again.

'It's a nice big Granada you've got in your drive. Wife has private money, does she?'

'Pools,' he grunted. Why didn't they ever think up anything better than that?

'How often do the pools come through?'

'Don't know what you're talking about.' This was getting tedious. Duffy flipped the Pause control and punched Gleeson again. Then he changed tack. Escalate quickly, that was one of his rules.

He sighed, strictly for Gleeson's benefit, picked up the hypodermic and held the point of the needle briefly in the candle flame. Then he made as if he was having second thoughts, turned towards the Castrol tin, and carefully rubbed the needle in the accumulated dirt round the pourer.

'You need it explained? I'll explain it. When we've finished, I'm going to use this spike to inject you. Now, as far as you've got a choice, here it is. This little bag,' he pointed at the polythene with the white powder, 'is, they assure me, ninety per cent pure. No, of course I didn't find it in the shed,' he replied to Gleeson's questioning glance, 'I went out and bought it. Now, I've only got their word for it, but as far as there are straight dealers, they've always proved straight. You might like to take a risk on how pure it is, but then again you might not.'

He let Gleeson puzzle at that for a while, then continued.

'If you feel you're unable to co-operate, or if you lie to me, or if you hold back, I'm going to inject this ninety per cent pure straight into your arm.' Which would kill you; he didn't need to tell him that. 'If you feel you can co-operate, then, when we've finished, I'm going to cut the smack with Marvel.' Which would make you feel you'd been hit with a sledge-hammer, but wouldn't actually kill you. 'Whether or not I drop the needle in the dirt a few times before I inject you depends very much on how I feel the evening's going.'

'You wouldn't kill me, Duffy.' There wasn't much bravado in the voice.

'I would kill you with no second thoughts.' What did another death on the route matter, especially that of someone who shifted the stuff? He said again, in a perfectly level voice, 'I would kill you with no second thoughts.' He left Gleeson to work out the angles, to imagine himself sitting roped to the chair, with a smear of blood on the inside of his forearm where the spike had come out, pop-eyed with fear, even after death. And the police would come, and they'd put it down as another small score being settled by someone on the heroin trail; and then they'd go into Gleeson's bank account, and then they'd watch Hendrick's shed for a while, but of course they wouldn't catch anything, and after a while they'd decide to keep it on file, which is another way of saying they'd wash their hands of it, and what did it matter anyway, just a fat pusher with mutton-chops roped to a chair, waiting for the dawn. It wasn't a nice death, either; you shitted yourself, you got a comic erection, you drowned in sweat. There was nothing to be said for it at all. Duffy's thumb flicked in his right-hand pocket.

'I didn't know what it was at first. I didn't, I swear I didn't.'

'How long ago was this?'

'About two years – two and a half years. One day Mrs Boseley comes up to me and says, "Would you mind delivering this case personally? I wouldn't want it to get lost on the way." It was something to go to Dude's. So I said fine – I like the driving, anyway. So I took it – I don't even remember what it was now – and I drove it to Dude's and forgot about it. And the next day Mrs Boseley gives me forty quid. Forty quid! "Just a little cash bonus, Gleeson, for delivering that case so well." Well, first of all I think, Christmas is early this year, then I think, Does she fancy me or something, then I sort of forget about it. Then it happens again, only this time it's fifty quid I get, and Mrs Boseley thanks me very nicely, and I think, Well if she does fancy me she's going a very funny way about it.

'The third time it happens I decide to ask. So after I've made the delivery I go to her office and say, "It's all right, what I'm doing, is it, Mrs Boseley?" and she says, "I'm very satisfied." And I say, "But, I mean, what is it I'm delivering?" and she says, "Are you sure you want to know?" and I think it over and I say, "No, I don't think so." And I say to myself, that's the last time you do this, Gleeson.

'And then a few months later Mrs Boseley tips me the wink again, and I say, "I think you'd better find yourself another driver," and she gets up and closes the door of her office. I remember her doing that. Then she sits down and says, "No, you're my driver, Gleeson." And I say, "I just resigned." And she says, "I'm afraid you can't." I say, "Why?" and she says, "Because I'd never find another driver as reliable as you," and I say, "Bullsh", or words to that effect, and she just says, "And in any case I can't let you." And it makes me feel there's something up. So I say, "Why not?" And she says, "Because you're in it now, like it or not. Stand or fall together," she says. I say, "What have I been taking to Dude's, then?" And she says, "Small amounts of heroin for medical purposes. Just small amounts; just for someone's old grandfather who became a heroin addict in China and has to get some stuff regularly, and the import regulations are so silly about it." And then she gives me a hundred pounds. In advance.'

Duffy hadn't heard the story before, but he'd heard the pattern of confession a million times – across an interrogation table, from the witness box, in a police cell. First it was I'm Just Mister Nice Guy; then it was Look What They Made Me Do. You wanted to say, if you *were* Mister Nice Guy you wouldn't have let Them Make You Do it. But that would be wasted breath. Duffy more or less believed Gleeson's story; at least, he didn't disbelieve him enough to hit him.

'Go on.'

'Well, it's sort of carried on from there. I just deliver. I just get paid for each run.'

It could be right, but Duffy didn't think so. There was always a first point at which a villain decides to halt his story. He thinks, they can't prove any more than that, so I'll stop there. That was what Gleeson was doing. Except that the circumstances were different. Duffy didn't have to prove anything. The burden of proof had shifted. Gleeson had to prove to Duffy that he'd told him everything he knew.

'And why was McKay crashed?'

'He was nicking things. He very nearly nicked the last shipment. By chance. We couldn't take the risk.'

Duffy picked up the knife and cut the lemon in half. He felt like a genteel tea-lady as he squeezed a little juice into the tablespoon. He looked across from the spoon to Gleeson. His guest didn't look at all happy.

'Go on.'

'Go on what?'

In response, Duffy tipped out the small amount of white powder from the polythene bag on to the saucer. Then he picked up the tin of Marvel, began to lever off the lid with the handle of the knife, seemed to have second thoughts, and banged the lid back down. Then, in case Gleeson got any ideas about sneezing or suddenly blowing hard, he put the spare saucer upside down over the one with the powder in it.

'Who, how, where, when?'

'There's only Mrs Boseley and Dalby, I don't know anyone else, Mrs Boseley doesn't tell me.' That was probably correct: heroin trails were normally run as tightly as possible. So Duffy merely said, for the tape's benefit as much as for the state of Gleeson's soul,

'And you.'

'And me. The stuff comes in about every three months or so. I take it to Mr Dalby.'

'Always?'

'Always. No one else.'

'And you deliver personally to him?'

'Yes. Mrs Boseley makes a call before I leave and he's always at the door when I get there.'

'Which door?'

'What do you mean, which door?'

'What does it look like, this door?'

'It's just a door, wooden door, says 61 on it.' Uh-huh; the back way, of course.

'And he pays you?'

'No, he just says, "Thank you, my fine fellow", or something snotty like that, and then shuts the door.' That was three of the four questions. Now the vital one.

'How?'

'How what?'

'How does it come through?'

Gleeson paused. Duffy unscrewed the plastic bottle and poured a small amount of water on top of the lemon juice. He could sense Gleeson's popping eyes following the operation.

'It varies. Sometimes it's in one thing, sometimes another. They never use the same system.'

'What is it next?'

'I don't know. Mrs Boseley knows.'

'How does Mrs Boseley know?'

'I don't know.' But he didn't sound confident about not knowing. Duffy picked up the tin of Marvel and put it down on the floor. On the other side of the packing-case. Where he might easily forget about it.

'It's marked on the air waybill number. There's always a double-four in them.'

Duffy got up and headed off towards Mrs Boseley's office. After a couple of steps he stopped, turned round, came back, lifted up the Castrol tin, waved it under Gleeson's nose, set it down again, and went off, all without a word. He returned with the file of invoices referring to Dalby's business, and with the file of forthcoming shipments.

'Show me.' He ran his finger down the first page until Gleeson nodded; then they went down every page in turn. All the shipments, as Gleeson had said, had a double-four in their air waybill number. Duffy opened the Forthcoming file. Again, he let Gleeson do the work, merely running his finger down until the nod came. It came very soon. 783/5236/144. One case tinned lychees. Port of origin: Hong Kong. Arrival date: Thursday. The day after tomorrow. No wonder they had been getting jumpy.

'That's the one?' said Duffy, and read the file number into the record.

'Yes.'

'And where's the heroin in them?'

'I don't know. They wouldn't tell me something like that. I wouldn't want to know anyway. It'll be somewhere in one of the tins, I suppose.'

'How many tins?'

'It's on the invoice.' Duffy showed him the file again and let

155

him do the reading. 'One gross eight-ounce tins of Chung Mon lychees.' Thanks very much. Duffy reached inside his right-hand pocket, switched the tape off, and began to get excited. Quite visibly so.

'Go on,' he said.

'Go on what?' The pitch of Gleeson's voice was rising with his panic.

Duffy began to warm the spoon over the candle.

'The rest, tell me the fucking rest, you scumbag.' His tone was getting a bit hysterical, though his hand wasn't shaking. It wasn't shaking either as he uncapped the saucer and carefully tipped half the white crystals into the spoon. Then he carried on warming it.

'There isn't any rest.'

But Duffy was scarcely listening to Gleeson any more. He was thinking about dead babies cut open and stuffed with bags of heroin and hurried over the border before they lost their natural colour. Dead babies who had to be under two years of age to be any use. Get past two and you're safe: you can grow up like any other kid. Grow up to be an addict if you feel like it, or a pusher; it's a free country.

And he was thinking about a serious-looking girl with dark hair and eyes which grew larger as her body wasted away. A girl intelligent enough to recognise that her own weakness of character was killing her. A girl with a carpet that smelt from her washed-out syringes. A girl he had run away from in case he found out what happened to her.

These two thoughts concentrated Duffy's mind wonderfully.

'There isn't any rest,' Gleeson whimpered. 'Mrs Boseley wouldn't tell me any more. I don't know where it comes from.'

Duffy stared at the dissolved liquid in the spoon. He didn't give a fuck about Gleeson, any more than Gleeson would have given a fuck about Lesley. Or any of them. He put down the spoon, and roughly wiped the dirt off the end of the hypodermic. He moved the tip towards the spoon.

'Marvel,' was all Gleeson said. Then again, softly, 'Marvel.'

Duffy put down the syringe, walked round the packing-case to where the powdered milk was, and kicked the tin very hard. Gleeson heard the tin land fifteen yards away, behind his back; then heard it roll for a while, hit something, and stop. That was the last he heard of the tin. His throat produced an involuntary squeak.

'There isn't any rest,' he repeated. He was speaking very softly, as if he feared the Castrol just as much as the hypodermic. Duffy dipped the end of the syringe in the solution and pulled back the plunger. The liquid was sucked smoothly up into the transparent plastic barrel of the hypodermic.

Briefly, Duffy laid the syringe down. He reached into his holdall and took out a pair of dressmaker's scissors and a piece of string. He sheared straight up Gleeson's right forearm, cutting through the jacket and the shirt at the same time. He pulled the flapping bits roughly back, and tied the string round his arm just above the elbow. He watched for a moment and saw the veins come up on the forearm. Gleeson still had good veins in his forearm, healthy, plump, fixable veins. Maybe he should fix Gleeson in the wrist, just below the handcuff. Or in the groin.

Duffy felt he was bursting. His ear throbbed. He picked up the hypodermic, held it at an upward angle, and pressed lightly on the plunger. The solution sprayed out in a fine curve, spotting the packing-case on which he had been sitting. He imagined the spray from Lesley's spike as she cleaned it out crazily on to her carpet. Then, with a sudden mental jump, he found himself remembering the spray from his cock as he sat downstairs in Dalby's crepuscular wankpit. Spraying up, out and over the carpet; just the same. Duffy felt excited; he felt a bit crazy.

The veins on Gleeson's wrist offered a wide choice. Duffy approached them. He held the arm down firmly with his left hand, and moved towards a broad, meandering vein with the tip of the needle. Gleeson passed out; his shifting weight nearly toppled the chair over sideways.

Duffy's ear hurt. His back hurt too. So did his hand; he was quite out of practice at punching people. He replaced the hypodermic and walked down the shed to where the tin of Marvel had landed. He picked it up, walked back and tucked it into his holdall. Then he put the other things back – the lemon, the bottle, the saucers, the full hypodermic. He unlocked the handcuffs and put them away. Then he untied Gleeson's feet. Now he was only loosely roped to the chair. Duffy waited for him to come round. It took about five minutes, but that didn't matter; Duffy needed time to recover as well.

Gleeson opened his eyes, and made his mutton-chops waggle as he shook himself back to consciousness. The first thing Duffy did was to turn round in front of him, haul up the back of his blouson, pull his shirt out of his jeans, and show him the tape recorder. Gleeson clearly couldn't work out why he wasn't dead; but Duffy didn't feel like giving him a hand with that one.

'Right,' he said. 'I've got all that, and I'd say, given the current attitudes of the judges, you'll get at least ten years. Unless you land a softy who might give you eight. Now, you've got two choices, the clever choice and the stupid choice. The stupid choice means that you don't do as I say, and as a result you get ten years, and Boseley and Dalby might just bugger off scot-free. The clever choice means that we get Boseley and Dalby and if we can wangle it that way, you get off; if they shop you, then you'll have to go down, but I'll speak up for you about how you came forward and volunteered information. You might get four or five.'

Duffy assumed that Gleeson would pick the clever way, and told him precisely what he expected of him. As he finished, he added,

'And by the way, just in case you're not happy with being clever, but want to get clever-clever, I'll have three copies of this tape made within an hour, and they'll all be on their way to different addresses.'

Gleeson nodded. He hadn't said anything at all since he saw the needle coming towards him. Duffy hoped he hadn't been struck dumb by the shock; he might be needed in the witness box, after all.

'The ropes are pretty loose,' he said as he walked off. 'Put the chair back where I found it, will you? Oh, and turn out the light on your way.'

Duffy drove fast to Bell's flat – not out of need, but out of exhilaration. He dumped the tape and left Geoff to get on with the copying and the distribution. Then he went back to his flat and unpacked his holdall. He squirted the contents of the hypodermic down the sink. Then he took out the polythene bag with the unused half of the crystals, and carefully, delicately poured them back into the salt cellar, where they belonged.

9

The first thing he did next morning was to ring Hendrick.

'Oh, it's Duffy, Mr Hendrick. Good news. I found the lighters.'

'You *what*?'

'I found the lighters. I was checking out the shed yesterday and I found them in the toilets. I reckon kids must have got in one dinnertime. They nicked a few, I'm afraid, but they're almost all there.'

'Good, Duffy, well *done*.'

'So I think we can say it was probably McKay.'

'I suppose we must conclude so. Poor fellow. He seemed so trustworthy too.'

'Yes, well, you never can tell, can you?' If McKay had had eight convictions for burglary and ten for handling, that would probably have made Hendrick trust him even more.

'No, you certainly can't.'

'So I'll get the lighters sent on, shall I, and we can call it a day. As a matter of fact I've managed to get myself the sack from Mrs Boseley, so it seems to be quite convenient all round.'

'Oh dear, I'm sorry to hear that, Mr Duffy, how did it come about?'

'Well, I think she probably did the right thing, to be honest. I wasn't really happy in my work.'

'Oh. Some of the chaps adore it, you know.'

'Yes, they've told me so.' He thought of Casey punching

him on the bicep with a 'Cun', herher'. 'So you'll get my bill in the morning, Mr Hendrick, and I hope you won't mind my mentioning that prompt settlement would be appreciated. These aren't easy days, as you doubtless know only too well yourself.'

'No, indeed. Well, thank you. Goodbye.'

Duffy dug out his Yellow Pages and looked up Food Importers. Three calls produced a near miss, a bugger off and a wrong number. He ploughed on. Eventually he got a yes: or rather, the three yesses he needed. Size, brand, and availability. Then followed two yesses of his own. Yes, a gross. Yes, he did have a lot of Chinese friends. And one no. No, he didn't need anything for the first course.

He collected them on his way to work. Sixty-five quid's worth of lychees rattling around in the back of the van. That put him in debt for the job, and he'd already spent – thoroughly spent – Gleeson's well-worn oncers. He supposed he could always eat some of them.

The man on the Cargo Terminal gate waved him through. Funny, there hadn't been any of those spot checks recently. He wondered why. A case of lychees wouldn't look all that probable, so he'd better take good care of the receipt from the Sino-Pak Food Company.

Dalby's shipment wasn't due until the next day, Thursday, but Duffy wasn't taking any chances. Freight had been known to arrive early, so he was covering that possibility.

But it didn't. Cockroach Airways were keeping to their schedule. '*All* 144 tins of lychees were killed,' Duffy began to himself, 'as a DC-10 . . . ' That would be ironic. He'd worried about friends going on planes before now – Carol going off for ten days in Sicily with Somebody – but never before about freight. Don't take off in the dark, he found himself whispering in the direction of Hong Kong.

The Wednesday was quiet. Duffy stayed out of Gleeson's way, stayed out of Mrs Boseley's way, even stayed out of Tan's way for no particular reason. He had his normally convivial lunch with Casey, and afterwards found himself nervously checking the back doors of his van. Yes, they were locked.

On the Thursday he rang Willett and Carol and asked them what their work schedules were over the next couple of days. Willett answered in a tone Duffy recognised: the tone that said, I'm not asking and You're not telling and You haven't made this call. Carol answered with a tone equally familiar to Duffy: the tone that said, Are you asking me round, Are you asking me out, and which sounded disappointed at the end when he rang off without being specific.

When he got to work he felt nervous. He parked his van half-way between the Terminal entrance and Hendrick Freight, down a little cul-de-sac leading to the shed of a now bankrupt forwarding agent. He walked to work and was overtaken on his way by Casey, who greeted him by hooting, accelerating savagely, mounting the pavement and swerving away at the last minute as Duffy thought he might have to jump on the bonnet or climb a twelve-foot wall.

'Gotcha,' said Casey as Duffy arrived in a state of irritated shock.

'Cun',' grumbled Duffy.

'Herher.'

The trouble was, for the next few hours it was up to Gleeson. They hadn't spoken since their evening in the shed; they'd barely looked at one another. The only outward sign that anything had happened was that Gleeson was wearing a different jacket from the one he normally came to work in. Duffy wondered how he'd explained that to his wife: the neatness of the cut, the slashing of the shirt as well. Still, that was the least of Duffy's problems. And certainly the least of Gleeson's.

At eleven Duffy found Gleeson tucked away behind a pile of cases, ticking off a list on his clipboard. Nobody else was in sight. Duffy passed the van keys over to him. A nasty thought crossed his mind, so he just said, quietly,

'The tapes came out really well.'

He left it at that and wandered back to his dunce's corner. For the rest of the day he paid no obvious attention to the running of the shed. He trundled his trolley, loaded and unloaded at command, made what was to be a farewell visit to the canteen with Casey, and kept his head down. The last thing he wanted to do was make Mrs Boseley suspect that he was in the slightest degree interested in a certain shipment from a certain part of the shed. Nor did he fancy getting ankle-tapped by a forkie at this stage. At two o'clock he tried very hard not to watch as Mrs Boseley bustled out of her glass hutch and spoke to Gleeson. Indeed, he deliberately went and fiddled in his locker so that he wouldn't see Gleeson fetch one of the company vans and back it up against a certain heap of newly arrived freight.

But after that, he couldn't keep his mind off what was meant to be happening. Gleeson would be backing up the cul-de-sac about now. He'd be opening the van doors. He'd have to make his decision *now*. The one decision Duffy had to leave to Gleeson, as he couldn't foresee how Dalby's lychees would be packaged. Gleeson either had to switch the documentation on to the case that Duffy had bought, or he had to open both cases laboriously, and transfer one gross of tinned lychees in each direction. And not drop one particular tin (which in the circumstances he wouldn't recognise, or get careless halfway through.

Now he was driving down the M4. Mind that lorry. Mind that bridge where McKay got crashed. Mind that bus. Mind that tricycle. Mind that cockroach. Careful that pigeon doesn't shit on the windscreen. Looks like rain – put your wipers on, Gleeson, *wipers*. Don't jump those lights. Smoothly. Mind that policeman. Well done, here we are, Number 61. Ring the bell, grovel as usual, hand it over, tug the mutton-chop deferentially to Mr Dalby, that's right, back in the transit. Careful on the way back – you've still got my van keys on you. Nothing fancy. Change down into third. Yes, doing well. Through the gate. Into the shed. Disengage gear; handbrake; ignition. Brill.

Gleeson walked over to Duffy and from a distance of a foot or so flung the van keys at him quite hard. Perhaps on the way back he'd been thinking of an angle Duffy hadn't mentioned to him: what if Dalby discovers straight away that he hasn't got what he thought he'd got? Duffy had his answer ready, just in case. It would obviously take Dalby a while, going through all those tins; and he might not do it till he got home, in any case. And then what would he find? The right tins, the right documentation, but no smack. He'd hardly pin that on the Heathrow courier; at least, not that quickly. He'd probably assume something had happened at the Hong Kong end.

But Dalby might be on the phone to Mrs Boseley sooner than anticipated. So Duffy decided it was time to sever his connection with Hendrick Freight. He sauntered up to the glass office and sat down opposite Mrs Boseley without being invited. She looked up: the high bones, the scraped-back hair, the cold, dead eyes. He found himself thinking, I hope you come out *grey*; I hope you come out fucked up; I hope you come out with nightmares which make you have to take little coloured pills and I hope you get hooked on them and eat more and more and lose weight until your polar eyes pop out of your face. Duffy didn't have a forgiving nature. But all he said was,

'Well, I'll be off now.'

'What?'

'I thought I'd be off now. Get out of your hair. Collect me cards. You can pay me off. I don't fancy coming back here tomorrow.'

'Nothing would give me greater pleasure.' She paid him, and gave him his cards. She seemed more relaxed now than at any time since he'd been in the shed. Yesterday she'd been jumpy – as well as very puzzled at the way he'd 'found' the cigarette lighters. Now she seemed, not exactly serene, but her normal self – dauntingly in control. He couldn't help taking a little stab at her as he left.

'By the way, Mrs Boseley, what's the E for?'

'I beg your pardon?'

'Is it Eva?'

She stared at him in an icily unamused manner.

'Elizabeth? Egbert? Ethelred? Eskimo?'

'It stands for Eff off, Duffy.'

He grinned at her as irritatingly as he could, and clattered down the stairs. When he got to the van he had an unpleasant thought. What if Gleeson had driven straight there? What if he had slipped away and was even now on his way out of the country or something? I mean, it wasn't exactly far to the airport, was it?

But the tins had been changed, and Duffy reflected how fanciful his anxiety had been: men like Gleeson didn't run. They didn't like abroad for a start. They'd rather sit in an English prison for a few years and read the morning paper and eat the local food than skip to some hot country where the grub was spiced and the natives unfriendly. Not that Duffy felt superior on this count: he'd rather take a long lease on an English cell than paddle in the wildest foreign luxury.

He drove home with care, absurdly solicitous about the welfare of the tins. He lugged them into the kitchen and put them on the drainer. He dug out his tin-opener and excitedly opened the first tin. Two lychees bobbed on the surface. He plunged in a forefinger and twirled it around. The fruit had an eerily smooth feel to them: it was like plunging your finger into a tin of eyeballs. He picked one of them up and bit into it. It had a fragrance as much as a taste: it was like eating the smell of roses. Duffy didn't much care for eating the smell of roses. He thought he was going to have a lot of tins left over at the end.

He was about to throw the first tin away when he had an unsettling thought. What if the heroin *had* been dissolved, as Willett suggested. What if it were swilling round in one of the tins, or several of the tins? That would screw things up. Depressed suddenly, he went on to the second tin. Then the third. On the fourth his fingers, sticky from probing the cans, slipped and the tin-opener skidaddled across the floor. Shit. This wasn't going to be an exercise which would leave him in a good mood.

He lined up the opened tins on the kitchen table in rows of ten. Ten, twenty, thirty. Duffy had seen enough lychees to last him a lifetime. Forty, fifty. Yet another good reason for not going abroad – cut down the chances of getting given lychees. Sixty, seventy. Duffy discovered his definition of hell: flying on a jumbo of Cockroach Airways and being fed meals of lychees. Eighty, eighty-six, eighty-seven. Uh-huh. Uh-HUH.

Beneath the three lychees bobbing on the surface of the syrup there was a package. Carefully, Duffy lifted out the three fruit and piled them on top of tin number eighty-six. Then he washed his hands. Then he laid out a double thickness of kitchen towel on the table next to tin number eighty-seven. He'd have put down a strip of red carpet if he'd had it handy.

He put in three fingers and lifted out a squat plastic bag. He laid it on the kitchen towel and held the tin up for inspection. There was a small tear at one point in the wrapper, and what seemed to be a pinprick in the curve of the 'g' of Chung Mon. No more than that, unless Duffy was missing something. From this direction, a pinprick in the lettering looked, well, almost obvious; but from the other angle, from the customs end? Duffy tried to imagine that as being their only clue in shipment after shipment of tinned goods. They'd be coming through regularly, month after month, and then suddenly there'd be a tin with a pinprick. What chance did Willett and his colleagues have?

Duffy swabbed the plastic package dry. It was fastened tightly at the top with thin wire. He removed the wire, and opened the top of the package. Another one was inside, upside down. He pulled it out; tied as tightly as the other, this time with string. Inside it, yet another bag, this time with a wire tie. Duffy imagined Carol's voice: Hey, Duffy, is that smack trying to escape? He smiled to himself. He looked inside the third bag, and there it was: lying contentedly, feeling safe. He licked a finger and tasted the fine white powder; it was bitter and salty. He closed the top. He weighed it in his hand; allowing for the three lychees put in as padding, and the juice, there were maybe six ounces here.

Then he went back to the cans. It was hard on the fingers. Maybe he should buy himself an electric can opener. No, maybe not: there can't be too many jobs like this. In can 117 he found another bag. He dug it out and put it on the kitchen roll beside the first one. Then he ploughed on. The rest of the cans proved, if only in one sense, fruitless. Finally, he stared at his kitchen table. One hundred and forty-four opened, dripping cans of lychees yawned back at him. It looked like one of those fairground games where you have to throw a ping-pong ball at a cluster of goldfish bowls: the ball bounces around the rims for a while, and if it falls into a bowl you win a prize. Duffy had won two.

He fetched two big black plastic refuse bags and poured all the lychees into one of them; then he threw all the tins (after carefully closing the lids) into the other. Then he mopped up the kitchen table, and changed the kitchen towel under the bags of heroin, as if it were a nappy. Then he sat down and stared at them for a while.

He was going to leave each portion in its own bag, until he remembered what Willett had told him. If by any chance the two bags had come from different factories, then that would screw things. Carefully, Duffy emptied their contents into a jam-jar. He shook it vigorously for a couple of minutes. Then he redistributed the heroin: he had six little plastic bags to share it among. Half he put back into one bag, which he tied with wire. The other half he distributed between the other five bags, and tied their tops. Shared out that way, they were only about half a centimetre deep when pressed down. That should do it.

He thoroughly washed the jam-jar and scrubbed the kitchen table. Then he had a thought. He reopened the black refuse bag which had the tins in it and took out a couple. He untied the wire from the top of Dalby's little package and dripped some of the lychee syrup into the heroin. That would ease things along a bit. Short of typing out arrest warrants, this was as helpful as Duffy thought he could be. If the Government Chemist was as shit-hot as Willett had said, he'd soon identify the liquid that had leaked into Dalby's smack. Oh yes, Mr Dalby, and did you on such-and-such a date take delivery of one gross of lychees? Duffy imagined Dalby's reply: Yes I did, and I opened every single one of them myself and *none* of them had my heroin in it. Thank you, Mr Dalby. The Crown rests its case.

Duffy put down his black bags on the way out to the van. He hoped the one with the fruit in it didn't burst. Seventy-odd pounds of sweet eyeballs rolling down the street, tasting of the smell of roses: that was all he needed. With relief he humped them into the back of his van. Then the tins. Then he pulled on his driving gloves and went back into the flat. He wiped the plastic packages very carefully and slipped the five slim packets into his right-hand blouson pocket. He could take Dalby's with him as well; but decided against it and put it in the fridge instead.

Last van to Fiddle City, he thought, as he idled along the M4. It was 9.30. The jumbos were back to being just coloured lights in the sky; as they hung there, scarcely moving, Duffy kept expecting them suddenly to go out, like the last trailing sparkles of a rocket. But they didn't. No, they wouldn't, would they, not as long as they had Duffy to annoy: that gave them a reason for living. And of course, all the pilots had decided to use the M4 route tonight. 'Well, I had thought about the North Circ, but I decided to waggle my wings at Duffy one last time – you know, suddenly lose a few hundred feet, cut the jets, and steer in his direction. He didn't like it much, you know. Swerved straight on to the hard shoulder and dived in a ditch. Funny fellow.'

At the shed it was quickly done. Third drawer down on the right, that was all he was interested in this visit. He unclipped the photo frame, and tucked the five thin bags in between the backboard and the photo of Dalby; then he did it up again. It was a bit tighter than before, but he doubted Mrs Boseley would notice. She would have eyes only for that plump English face, that sweet bald head, those cute little round gold glasses. When did she look at it, Duffy wondered: when the day was going well, or when the day was going badly? Why *did* people have photos on their desks? Duffy didn't know. Duffy didn't even have a desk.

Back at the flat he had a few more hours to kill. He rescrubbed the kitchen table, rewashed the jam-jar, ate a pork pie and sat watching television. The trouble was, he had to keep switching channels. He was enjoying a rerun of *North By Northwest* until it struck him that Eva Marie Saint was perfect for the part of Mrs Boseley. He button-punched away from a comedy duo because the fat one kept waggling his face around and Duffy only had to paint on a pair of mutton-chops to be with Gleeson. And then a forty-five minute BBC-2 film about a social worker, which Duffy was intensely bored by, but thought was entirely safe, suddenly blew up in his face during a case conference; one of the other social workers looked just like Lesley. He stopped watching television, rechecked Willett's and Carol's schedules, and tuned in to a late-night radio phone-in. It was all about the distribution of Britain's North Sea oil revenue, and proved harmless.

At one in the morning he stuffed the single bag of heroin into his blouson and set off. He'd had a long stare at the lock on the door of Number 61 and had marked off half a dozen keys to try first. He was fairly confident one of them would do the trick. He didn't fancy standing on the doorstep too long and hearing the distant tread of some keen young copper: some updated version of the younger Duffy. Attempted burglary while in possession of heroin didn't sound the sort of offence for which he'd get an unconditional discharge.

But the door yielded at the third key. Now all he had to hope was that Dalby wasn't romancing one of his employees, wasn't taking a post-coital header into the tub at this very moment. The office was empty; the bedroom behind was empty; out of curiosity Duffy looked at the bath. Hmm, looked just like a normal bath; disappointing. He took the bag of heroin out of his blouson pocket and had a think. Then it came to him. Where might plump little Englishmen put their treasures? Where childhood's magic used to unfold. Duffy tucked the bag of heroin underneath Dalby's pillow. The tooth that once fell out could turn into a sixpence. The heroin could turn into thousands of dreams, thousands of sensations, millions of sixpences. It could also turn into some dead people. Or, in this case, it could turn into a long prison sentence.

He left Dalby's office and looked down the few steps at the wankpit. The candles and the joss-sticks were dead, the champagne and the spunk in the carpet were slowly drying out. The smell of it was pretty bad, even from here. You probably would want to take a lot of baths if you ran a place like this. He thought of his hand, wet from the champagne bottle, being politely reapplied to the girl's nearer breast. 'You can hold them,' she'd said. 'You've paid for them. They're not for looking at.' Duffy turned and left.

At eight o'clock the next morning he made the first of two phone calls.

'W.P.C. Lucas, please,' he said in a strong Welsh accent.

'Carol, some Taff for you,' he heard a voice shout, while a hand was inefficiently cupped over the mouthpiece.

'Hallo?'

'*Don't* say my name, it's Duffy. Or rather, it's your anonymous Welsh informer. That place I made you sit outside the other night – Dude's. I'd say there might be some heroin in there somewhere. The fellow probably uses it just before he goes to bed, or maybe when he's in bed.' He told her where Dalby's private door was, so that the ferrets could start at both ends. 'Oh, and your anonymous Welsh informer will be ringing you next week about a celebratory meal.'

'Oh, D . . .'

'*Don't* say my name.' Christ, she'd nearly blown it then. 'I mean, we're not necessarily going out' (after all, he'd taken her out only recently) 'but we could stay home. I could cook you something. I'll learn a new takeaway.'

'Thank you for your information,' replied Carol correctly.

Then he rang Willett and directed him, without being too specific, towards the task of ripping Mrs Boseley's desk apart, and preferably her with it. After he'd rung off, he regretted he hadn't just said, 'There's half of it in the photograph frame, and half of it up Mrs Boseley's bum.' That would have made her eyes swivel.

He hung around the flat for a bit, not knowing what to do. He didn't want to be around when the raids took place. Certainly not there, and not even here, at the end of a telephone. One of the troubles was, he could never leave a ringing telephone unanswered. If only he could train himself to do that, he could sit around the flat all the time.

What did other people do when they had nothing to do, Duffy wondered. Visited their old mums or something, he supposed. Duffy didn't have an old mum. But he had one small thing to do, at least. He drove round the North Circular for a few miles, turned off into a stretch of London which was being slowly gentrified, and found himself a skip. He dumped the lychees and the tins. Then he bought himself a pub lunch.

He drove slowly home and called at a couple of kitchen shops on the way. He bought some plastic bags in the one size he was getting a bit low on. There didn't seem to be anything else he wanted to buy. Carol had this picture of him as someone who kept squirrelling away kitchen equipment. Duffy thought this was unfair; he just wanted to have enough of everything. He hated the idea of running out.

Why didn't he feel excited, he wondered, at the end of this job? It *was* the end, after all: Carol and Willett would struggle briefly with their consciences, would worry a bit over whether Duffy had just been very smart or whether he'd been fiddling things, but would accept what they'd been given; hell, they might even get commended for their smart cultivation of contacts – so why should he worry? And as for his methods: well, Duffy thought, when in Fiddle City . . .

Even so, the job did leave him feeling depressed. Depressed at the thought of a world which had dead babies at one end of it, dead girl fixers at the other, and in the middle a swarm of tireless operators who just sat around for a few months, and then, with a pinprick in a tin label, did what they wanted to and got away with it. He was depressed, too, at parts of his own reaction to it all: for instance, at the way he'd wanted to kill Gleeson. He realised soberly that he might very well have done so if he'd had the real thing in his syringe.

Well, there weren't any new methods of stopping feeling depressed; there were only the old methods. He spruced himself up and headed off to the Alligator. He got there right on opening time, six o'clock. He drank double whiskys, not very fast, but fast enough. It wasn't so much that after a while he began to stop feeling depressed; it was more that he started to feel very drunk. At nine o'clock there was a shuffle at the next barstool and a cough.

'My dear Sir Duffy.'

He turned. Slowly, don't overshoot the stool. Uh-HUH:

'Eric.' It was that Eric fellow. Why had Duffy thought of him as unhealthy-looking? He'd never seen a fitter man in his life. He looked very healthy. He looked very neat. He looked very nice too.

'Drink for my friend,' Duffy shouted in what he judged to be more or less the direction of the barman.

'I knew I'd win one day,' said Eric, and ordered a triple vodka and tonic. 'These bar measures,' he said to Duffy by way of explanation. Christ, Duffy did look drunk. He should have ordered a quadruple.

'Well, Sir Duffy, what have you been up to today?'

'Ah,' replied Duffy, and turned back towards the bar, partly out of modesty at his exploit and partly so as to hold on better. 'I caught Lord Lucan today.'

Eric winked at the barman as his drink arrived.

'Another triumph for Duffy Security. How did you manage that?'

'Well, you see . . . ' (Christ he really *was* pissed) 'he was flying this jumbo b'longing to Crock . . . to Cook . . . to Cruc . . . to Cockr . . . '

'To *who*?'

But Eric never found out. Duffy suddenly keeled over into his arms, knocking Eric's triple vodka to the floor as he did so. With the help of the barman, Eric hauled him back on to his stool. Duffy was very heavy, pulling his full drunk's weight. Briefly, he opened an eye, and smiled seraphically across at Eric. His lips fumbled their way into action.

'Your round, I think.'

ABOUT THE AUTHOR

Dan Kavanagh was born in County Sligo in 1946. After an uncompromising adolescence, at nineteen he became assistant entertainments officer on a Japanese supertanker and traveled the world. He has been a pianist in a waterfront bar in Macao, a baggage handler at San Francisco Airport, and has flown light planes on the Colombian cocaine route. He is currently working in London at jobs he declines to specify, and lives in North Islington. He is also the author of *Duffy*.

***Other mysteries you'll enjoy from
the Pantheon International Crime series:***

Peter Dickinson

"Sets new standards in the mystery field that will be hard to live up to."
— Ruth Rendell

Death of a Unicorn	74100	$3.50
Hindsight	72603	$2.95
The Last Houseparty	71601	$2.95
King and Joker	71600	$2.95
The Lively Dead	73317	$2.95
The Old English Peep Show	72602	$2.95
The Poison Oracle	71023	$2.95
Sleep and His Brother	74452	$3.95
Walking Dead	74173	$3.95

Reginald Hill

A Killing Kindness   71060 $2.95

"A cause for rejoicing....Sparkles with a distinct mixture of the bawdy and
the compassionate." — Robin W. Winks, *New Republic*

Who Guards the Prince?   71337 $2.95

Cornelius Hirschberg

Florentine Finish   72837 $2.95

"A crackerjack murder tale, swift, well-handled, well-written."
— *Saturday Review*

Dan Kavanagh

Duffy   74442 $3.95

"Exciting, funny, and refreshingly nasty." — Martin Amis

Fiddle City   74441 $3.95

"The snap and crackle of Raymond Chandler." — *Book Choice*

Hans Hellmut Kirst

The Night of the Generals   72752 $2.95

"One of the finest detective novels from any source in many years."
— *New York Times Book Review*

Hans Koning

Dewitt's War   72278 $2.95

"I recognize in this book all the subtlety of my fellow writer Koning."
— Georges Simenon

Norman Lewis

Cuban Passage   71420 $2.95

Flight from a Dark Equator   72294 $2.95

"A beautifully staged safari into the nature of evil in faraway places."
— *New York Times Book Review*

Peter Lovesey

The False Inspector Dew   71338 $2.95

"Irresistible...delightfully off-beat...wickedly clever."

       —*Washington Post Book World*

Keystone   72604 $2.95

James McClure

"A distinguished crime novelist who has created in his Africaner Tromp Kramer and Bantu Sergeant Zondi two detectives who are as far from stereotypes as any in the genre."   —P.D. James, *New York Times Book Review*

The Artful Egg	72126	$3.95
The Blood of an Englishman	71019	$2.95
The Caterpillar Cop	71058	$2.95
The Gooseberry Fool	71059	$2.95
Snake	72304	$2.95
The Sunday Hangman	72992	$2.95
The Steam Pig	71021	$2.95

William McIlvanney

Laidlaw   73338 $2.95

"I have seldom been so taken by a character as I was by the angry and compassionate Glasgow detective, Laidlaw. McIlvanney is to be congratulated."   —Ross MacDonald

The Papers of Tony Veitch   73486 $2.95

Poul Ørum

Scapegoat   71335 $2.95

"Not only a very good mystery, but also a highly literate novel."

       —Maj Sjöwall

Martin Page

The Man Who Stole the Mona Lisa   74098 $3.50

"Full of life and good humor....His novel is a delight."   —*New Yorker*

Julian Rathbone

"Right up there with Le Carré and company."   —*Publishers Weekly*

A Spy of the Old School	72276	$2.95
The Euro-Killers	71061	$2.95

Vassilis Vassilikos

Z   72990 $3.95

"A fascinating novel."   —*Atlantic*

Per Wahlöö

Murder on the Thirty-First Floor   70840 $2.95

"Something quite special and fascinating." —*New York Times Book Review*

Elliot West

The Night Is a Time for Listening   74099 $3.95

"The major spy novel of the year."   —*New York Times*